HERE

Ella James

ISBN-13: 978-1479124541
ISBN-10: 1479124540

For Peggy

CHAPTER ONE

The day it happened, things were regular enough.
Halah, Sara Kate, and Bree had spent the night—a chilly October Friday we'd talked through until the sun rose, pink and soft across the Rockies. I awoke to Sara Kate's knee in my back, sharp enough to poke a hole through my favorite Cream t-shirt. Halah and Bree were curled up on the floor, Halah's pink subzero "hotsack" tossed over the Miley Cyrus bag Bree's grandmother had given her the previous Christmas—the year we'd turned 15. Halah called the bag Miss Miley, and at sleepovers at Sara Kate or Halah's house, I usually fought Bree for her.

This morning, Halah's curly head stuck up, and her hazel eyes met mine. We grinned, then pounced on Bree, chanting "Miss Miley, Miss Miley, Miss Miley!" till Bree lurched up, her curvy body raining fragments of the popcorn we'd all munched and, later, crunched into my rug.

"Shhh*hhh!*" That was Sara Kate, lumbering up and glaring at us. She was never a morning person, and she'd been even less one since she'd started hanging out with Ami McVea of the multi-colored dreadlocks and **Turn Off Your Radio** (KILL THE MACHINE) bumper sticker. S.K. hadn't actually told me this—I was only her best friend, after all—

1

but I'd overheard her talking to Ami after orchestra practice, saying something about midnight rides, and I happened to know from my college cousin West that Ami and S.K. had been sneaking out on weeknights, riding into Denver to go to (what else?) indie music shows.

"You're riding with the big dawgs. This ain't no rusty banged up Beetle," Halah drawled. She had the most ridiculous faux Old West accent ever, and she was referencing Ami McVea's VW bug. We—the quad—had called ourselves the big dogs in years past, although I couldn't quite remember why.

Bree ambled over and barked in Sara Kate's ear. S.K. batted her off, then slid out of my bed and pulled a Pop Tart out of her overnight bag. Halah braided Bree's hair, and S.K. painted her toenails with my electric lilac polish, and I straightened my room and made us waffles, which we ate on the downstairs couch, watching *Jeopardy* re-runs that Halah killed, 'cause that girl made awesomesauce out of random facts, despite what she wanted our school to think. (Re: brainless, badass, and beautiful).

Half an hour later, the four of us stood in the pebbly indention of my driveway, a time-shorn path through the rough grass that dusted the foothills of the mountains.

I looked at Bree and Halah, a unit within our unit, best friends just like S.K. and me. "You guys be careful." I smiled tightly. "Halah, spare Bobby the crotch shot."

Bobby Malone was this senior who'd cheated on one of Halah's cheer teammates—Annabelle Monroe, the blonde cheerleader archetype. Which is why he was also the bull's eye in the day's paintball meet-up.

Halah grinned wickedly. "I'm not going for his crotch,

Milo. I'm going for his little tiny *balls*."

"That's disgusting." Bree's nose scrunched.

"Keep her out of trouble, mkay?"

Bree shrugged. She had a piece of popcorn smashed under her breasts.

"I want pictures," S.K. called, as Hal and Bree set off.

"Only if they can't be used against us in a court of law," Halah called back.

They drove away, aiming for the far-off fence at the front edge of Mitchell property. Hang a left, and they'd be on a gravel road that ran below the massive Front Range, just a tiny ribbon if viewed from the top of the peaks, up by turbines.

Mitchell Turbines.

Mitchell Windfarm.

Home.

S.K. was never much for goodbyes, and after all, we didn't know that's what this was. That bright gray morning was just an ordinary Saturday, on an ordinary weekend in our junior year at Golden Prep, the only private arts high school on our side of Denver.

"Have fun with Bambi," she said, and tossed her black hair, like the glossy, perfect mane annoyed the heck out of her. (For the record, it really did).

"Have fun with Jackie Chan."

That would be her Tae Kwon Do instructor, a big, smiling hottie whose actual name was David.

S.K. arched one brow. It jutted up over the frames of her black, square-ish glasses.

"Sayonara," she said.

And that was that.

My plan for the afternoon involved a dart gun, a tracking bracelet, and my beat-up copy of *The Great Gatsby*.

I had a seasonal reading plan I'd stuck with each year since fifth grade: *Walden* in the spring, *Pride & Prejudice* in the summer, *The Great Gatsby* each fall, and *Wuthering Heights* every winter (my dad's dad, Gus Mitchell, had been a tenth-grade English teacher). I liked to imagine the rock-strewn, fir-dotted fields that rolled out toward the mountain range as my moors. In the privacy of my favorite woodsy spot, I savored my cold-weather reading with a gusto that made me feel like a walking liberal arts student cliché.

With *Gatsby* in my pack and the dart gun in my gloved fist, I drifted through the fields, watching fir needles tremble, tracking birds as they rose and fell, formed flocks and scattered. They'd be leaving in the next month, before it got too cold for anything sans fur.

I wondered if my herd of mule deer would already be there: by the creek that threaded through the northeast edge of our land. I hoped not. If they were waiting, I couldn't sneak up on them. Encroaching winter made it especially important that I tag the last of the year's fawns—*now*. When the snow came, their grazing patterns changed. The creek would ice over and the herd would scatter, seeking out the Bancrofts' hot springs or one of the freeze-proof waterfalls just north of our property, on the land owned by Mr. Suxley.

As I walked, arms stuck in the pockets of my dad's giant hunting coat, I thought back over the night. I was a cataloguer of events, but like too many other times lately, I felt like I didn't have enough to file. I seemed to be moving at a different pace from all my friends. Halah—Halah with her unabashed love of Martin Lawrence movies and her closet full of oversized softball t-shirts—had shot off, three light years ahead of me. She had a senior boyfriend on the wrestling team, and she didn't have a curfew.

Bree was just... Bree. I didn't even have a scale for how she and I compared. While I thought about everything ad nauseum, Bree never seemed to think about anything that wasn't practical. The week before, she'd spent half of lunch on her phone trying to find the area's best dry-cleaner.

And then there was S.K. Sara Kate, my best friend. My other half. My favorite person on the planet—other than my dad, who wasn't on the planet anymore. S.K. who'd gone with (guess who?) Ami to ComicCon the weekend of my birthday. Who'd recently decided she needed more time to herself. "I'm getting too stressed out by all this *stuff*." Stuff being me. The quad. Our fun.

Lately, the thing I liked best about this deer gig was how *somewhere else* it made me feel. With the sky over my head and the grass crunching under my boots, I could be anywhere. Add a book to the equation, and I wasn't Milo Mitchell, girl pianist, airheaded over-thinker, tenth-grade chemistry straggler, secret wallflower, lover of anime. I was Catherine. Well... maybe someone slightly less insane. Daisy Buchanan? Okay, someone moderately less shallow. Haruhi Suzumiya.

Made-up (and insane!) though they were, those people knew what they were about. Knew what they wanted. Whereas me... I got my kicks sedating mule deer.

I pointed myself left, toward the mountains, and picked up my pace for the last half-mile to the pine grove. There was a bluff oak right at the front of the grove, beside a big pancake-looking boulder; next to the skinny evergreens, it resembled a pom-pom in mid-cheer.

When I was growing up, this had been my dad's favorite spot. He and mom had come to Colorado to build the turbines—Mitchell Wind Turbines, his own patented design—but his real passion was outdoors stuff. As a little girl, I'd gone tromping through the fields and scaling cliffs with him. He'd taken me to Yellowstone and Grand Teton, Death Valley and Yosemite, but he'd really loved to take mc to the bluff oak.

"It's an anomaly," I could hear him say. "Supposed to be down South. Not out here with all the firs."

And yet, it was.

I walked under its limbs and stared down at the etched stone marker:

Faulkner Dursey Mitchell
1964-2010

And then, under that, in tiny, sharp-edged caps:

IN WILDERNESS, THE PRESERVATION
OF THE WORLD

I didn't like the marker, though I knew my dad had chosen it. In his absence, I'd grown irritated with the message. Preservation. What a stupid concept. My father wasn't preserved under the headstone. He was gone, and he was becoming more and more gone all the time.

Still, that didn't stop me from my pilgrimage. Since that awful day almost two years ago, I'd visited the marker and the bluff oak often. Actually, I'd treated this place like Mecca until two months ago.

It had been the first Saturday after school had started. S.K. spent the night but left early the next morning for her first date with Ami. Halah was at a cheer retreat, and Bree was... somewhere. I don't remember.

I'd left at the same time as S.K., and by the time I got to the pancake boulder I was falling asleep on my feet. I took a nap—the boulder was that flat—but maybe an hour later, I was jerked awake.

I felt like someone was over me—I felt the hairs raise on the back of my neck. I rolled off the rock and jumped to my feet, ready to bolt. But no one was there. I ducked a second later, because I felt it again, and then I yelped. A needle pricked where my head met my neck, and the pain was inside my *brain*.

The terrifying thing was, it felt invasive. Like someone was reading my diary—while I stood naked in front of my class.

I left immediately, and spent the walk home freaking out. But I found my way back the next day. And felt the same thing. It wasn't as sudden, or as potent, but the feeling, like I was being *measured*, was still there.

And it was there Wednesday, when I went back after half a week: that stripped-down-to-the-cells, stuck-under-a microscope, known-inside-and-out, freaky deaky looked-through feeling. Was I hallucinating? The last thing I needed was another mental health issue to deal with. Obviously, I needed to find another way to feel close to Dad.

After a lot of working myself up to it, I called the Department of Conservation and Wildlife, posed as my

7

mother, and got permission to continue Dad's mule deer tracking project.

I had all his old folders, stuffed with diagrams and data, so it hadn't been hard to figure out who was who among the herd. After that, it was just a matter of coming out on Saturdays and tagging them.

It was easy to shoot the sedative gun, bring the deer down, and snap a bracelet over their hard, dark hooves. I spent my weeknights, after studying, watching the gob of blinking lights move across my laptop screen. I knew where they slept and where they roamed. I knew where they went mid-afternoon: the creek.

I made my way over to it now, crunching over fallen leaves from the seasonal trees that blazed orange, yellow, and red between the firs.

I heard the creek before I saw it, a gentle tinkling like a bowl of glass marbles pouring out. The smell of dirt and pine filled my nose and throat. The cold air whipped my cheeks. The sunlight swirled in spirals over the leaf-strewn bank. I thought about *Gatsby* and felt a dorky burst of excitement. I was right at the start of Chapter 9—the last chapter. I'd gone through the book too fast.

Reading the end made me feel either bursting full or empty. I walked faster, hoping this would be a day that I could enjoy the story without letting it gnaw at me. Otherwise it was going to be a long afternoon.

The tree house hung above a bend in the creek. Dad and I selected the strongest tree for its base: a horse-chestnut on the opposite bank. To get to it—if I didn't want to wade through chilly, waist-deep water—I had to climb a spiral staircase around a buckeye tree and sway across the rope-

and-board bridge we made the summer after second grade.

The wooden stair rails were cold, even through my gloves. I slid my palms over the ropes and crossed the sanded cedar planks. Waiting for me on the other side, the tree house was a thatch-roofed dome attached to the chestnut's trunk by beams that angled peaceably through its branches.

I pushed through the small door, surprised, as always, by how pretty it was here. The walls were warm cedar, and my Dad had built a bench that wrapped around the circular room. We used to get new cushions every year, but the green and red plaid we'd put out two Christmases ago would probably stay until the years ate through them. I had no plans to replace them.

I found my binoculars in the box where I'd left them, along with a blanket, a tin tub of almonds, and a little pile of air-activated hand-warmers.

I sat my pack down, grabbed the binoculars, and shed my gloves. Much as I wanted to stay warm, I couldn't fire the darts with padded fingers.

I gave myself a few minutes inside the house, designed with small gaps in the floor for circulation, but no windows (to hold heat in). Then I stepped back onto the bridge and sat with my back against the door. My gaze roved the forest, stopping at stray branches, odd-shaped stumps—anything that remotely resembled deer. Too early. I'd spotted them this morning near Mr. Suxley's woods, where they sometimes bedded down. It would take a little while for them to reach the creek.

I read. Nick Carraway, meeting up with Tom downtown. Leaving the West Egg. I sipped warm water from a metal thermos and tried not to think about my hunger, which couldn't be satiated in nose-range of the deer. The sun climbed higher, raining a kaleidoscope of golden light over Dad's bulky suede jacket and my camo pants. As I read, my hair sparkled in my periphery, a blanket of glossy brown, with red highlights glinting in the sun. I blew into my balled-up hands. Applied a scentless beeswax Chapstick.

I couldn't warm up. I cursed, Klingon swear words S.K. and I had looked up in sixth grade. Tracking deer was a terrible idea. I could be playing paintball.

I flipped to my favorite scene.

"Gatsby believed in that green light, the orgiastic future that year by year recedes before us. It eluded us then, but that's no matter—tomorrow we will run faster, stretch out our arms farther... And one fine morning—So we beat on, boats against the current, borne back ceaselessly into the—"

I heard a loud crunch, and my eyes leapt from the page. Blitzen! The herd's largest male had a star-shaped scar across his shoulder and a weathered coat. He stood by a holly bush ten or fifteen yards away, sniffing the air, his nostrils snorting out puffs of steam. Right behind him was Madonna, the alpha female, and then Brutus, a younger male who sometimes challenged Blitzen. Soon they were all there, including little Ashlyn, one of the youngest fawns, and my target.

Crap!

I should've been crouching, but I hadn't expected them until closer to four. Since there was no way I could sight Ashlyn—or any of them—from my spot flat on my butt, I stood slowly and ducked through the bridge's two rail-ropes, rising into a sort of squirrel-eating-nut position, with my arms up near my face and my feet balancing on the edge of the cedar planks. A lesser woodswoman might have fallen, or scared the deer, but I'd been doing this for years.

My fingers folded, steady, around the handle of the gun. I leaned my head down, peering through the sight. A breeze rocked the bridge; the rope above my head brushed against the top of my hair. My body felt pinched. Stiff. And then, finally, I had her. Ashlyn side-stepped, her small flank bumping into teenage Aiden's long, strong throat. Aiden strode forward, and there!

In the moment that the dart shot out, I felt a rush of pure elation. As it sailed toward little Ashlyn, I watched the frozen herd, processing the milliseconds till the dart would hit, Ashlyn would fall, the rest would bolt.

But that's not how it happened.

As my breath puffed out, creating a pale cloud that lent the scene a gauzy haze, I felt a bite of what could only be described as shock. My limbs and torso locked; my lungs went still. There was a flash of golden light, like a solar flare, except for one protracted second it was all there was. All there ever would be.

Then it receded, twisting the trees' shadows, mangling the forest floor. The creek spilled forth on fast forward. My blood boomed like a gunshot in my ears.

I searched for Ashlyn's body, but she wasn't there. A boy was.

CHAPTER TWO

He lay just beside the water, curled over on his side with his arms around himself and his knees drawn to his chest. From my perch up on the bridge, I could see he had hair the color of burnt rust and looked about my age.

When I thought about it a little later, I figured I must have been seriously freaking out, because as I stared down at him, the world seemed to stretch and rip—a kaleidoscope twisting in furious fingers. The air crackled like a huge branch snapping, and the pressure squeezed my eardrums, announcing the End of both our lives and the Beginning of something unimaginably new.

The really awful thing is: all I could think about was *Twilight*.

I'd become book critic enough to know the story's flaws, but when I'd gotten the series for Christmas in the seventh grade, I'd liked the vampire-werewolf fantasy better than I had ever admitted to my friends (even S.K., who was herself a fanatic). Which meant animals that occasionally turned human seemed real enough to me.

Staring down at the felled boy, my mind spun like a Ferris wheel. Had I accidentally hit Aiden instead of Ashlyn? Were my mule deer really mule guys and mule girls?

A violent breeze swept through the woods, shaking the bridge, and reality returned in a burst of sickening fright.

"Holy freaking baktag! Holy *shit!*"

I'd shot a *person!*

My legs jolted into motion before I was ready; I bumped into the bridge's rope handrails and shrieked, then shot off toward the stairs, practically fell down them.

"Hey!" I sprinted to him, dropping to the damp sand. "HEY! Are you okay?!"

I shook his shoulder. His head lolled back, bright copper curls pressed into the sand. His eyes were shut, his chiseled lips parted.

"Oh, *God*. Can you hear me? Please talk to me!"

I rocked back, cradling my head. Could a dart calibrated for a small fawn kill a guy my age? I didn't know. I didn't know much about the dart gun. I wasn't even supposed to be using it!

My breath came in frantic tugs, like I was breathing for him and me. I looked down at him again and felt the ground below me tilt.

The boy's curls looked afire against the dull wool of his tux. I followed the crisp lines of fabric down to his abs, where—*oh, God*—the dart's tail stuck out of a swatch of inky fabric.

My hand hovered over it.

"Oh, God. Oh God."

What if he never woke up? Should I be calling 9-1-1? I fumbled in my pants pocket for my phone—But wait! I didn't have service here!

Jerky like a wind-up doll, I leaned over his body and splayed my palm across his cheek. It was creamy—not pale or flushed—and to me it looked unnaturally perfect. He didn't have a single blemish. Not even a freckle. I wiggled my fingers, tap-tapping on his cheek below his eye. "Hey... c'mon. Talk to me!"

My hands were shaking too much to check his pulse at the wrist, but I was able to press my fingers against his jugular, digging in to find the heartbeat at his throat.

Slow but steady.

"Okay." I huffed. "Okay." I sucked air through my nose, let it out slowly through my mouth. A shrink had taught me this. Dr. Sam, the guy my mom sent me to after Dad died and I had my—well, my issues. "Okay."

I needed to practice what Dr. Sam had called positive projection.

This guy will wake up soon. This guy will wake up soon. And when he does he will be fine. When he does he will be fine.

His neck was warm and firm, with a muscular quality that reminded me a little of an animal. The dart was only supposed to put a mule deer out for a few minutes, so it couldn't take much longer for a human. *Could it?*

No, Milo. Of course it can't.

The mental tricks did their job. I was able to calm down enough to think, and the first thing I thought was that I needed to examine him more closely. I stared down at him, noticing minute things, like the poet-or-surfer curliness of his brilliant, bronzy hair. How thick and soft it looked, like a thousand loosely curving ocean waves. His shoulders seemed unusually wide, but maybe that was the tux.

Wait—

Why the heck was he wearing a *tuxedo*? I glanced

around, half expecting Bond-like reinforcements, but all I saw were leaves and branches. Our land was isolated. Fenced. So where on Earth had he come from?

I looked back at his face: his parted lips, the sharp line of his jaw, the gentle plane of his nose, the way his lashes fanned against his cheek.

A pristine white hanky poked out of his breast pocket, folded so harshly it looked fake. My gaze swept down his long legs before I realized I was—oh, no—gawking, and forced my attention back up to his face.

Coloring: good. Eyelids: unmoving. Mouth: not frothing or bleeding or bruised. In the last three years, I'd become an expert on vital signs, and my throat flattened a sob as I realized how familiar this routine felt.

I grabbed his hand and squeezed my eyes shut. *He's not dead, Milo.* I'd felt his pulse. Now I simply had to wake him up.

Pressing his warm hand between both of mine, I leaned down and spoke loudly near his ear. "Okay, now. It's time to GET UP."

I held my breath, gritted my teeth, and willed his eyes to open.

And they did. No fluttering lashes or painful squints or groans. He simply opened his eyes and blinked, just like an owl.

His eyes were deep brown. Wide and slightly glazed, they held mine like a magnet. Then he rolled onto his back, kicked out one long leg, and grimaced as he pulled the dart from his chest. He held it up into the sunlight.

Words gushed out of my mouth. "I'm sorry! Are you *okay*? I'm sooo sorry. I was trying to shoot a deer and you just—" what? He'd just *appeared*.

Except—okay—that clearly wasn't what actually happened.

The boy's rust-smudge brows clenched.

"I shot you!" I blurted. "That's a dart!"

He turned the tiny pink dart over in his hand. His mouth tightened, and I felt sure he was going to say something along the lines of, *My father the Congressman will be sure you're prosecuted to the fullest extent of the law.*

Instead, the corners of his mouth curved slowly. He sat up fully, leaning back on one arm, and in a rich, black-coffee kind of voice, he said, "You shot me?"

He was grinning and, a second later, laughing. His shoulders shook, his head lolled back. The sound of it was uproarious. Wonderful. As was his dark gaze, affixed to mine. "You *shot* me?" The words puffed out on hoots of laughter. "And you were aiming for a deer?"

He laughed so long I felt my cheeks color.

"You might consider wearing orange in the woods," I advised, wiping my hair back. "Anything with some color. Your hair's not *that* red, and black and white don't really say 'I'm human.'"

"What do they say?" His grinning face was lit up like a Christmas tree.

"I don't know…" Against my will, I felt my own lips twitch. I glanced over his tux. "Nick Carraway?"

He considered that for a second. "*The Great Gatsby*?"

"Yeah."

"He's human. Or would be if he was real." Still smiling that brilliant smile, he raked a hand back through his hair, trailing down over his face and over his jacket. Slowly, the smile faded. He looked down at himself for so long I forgot to breathe.

"Um... Hey," I said. "Are you okay?"

He looked at me like he'd forgotten I was there. His mouth was pinched tight now, his brown eyes flat.

"Do you feel bad?" I asked; my voice quivered.

My victim shook his head. "No." His mouth moved slowly, as if testing out the word. "I don't feel...bad."

"Are you sure?" I was leaning forward now, hands clenched in my lap.

"I don't know." The words were mumbled, like he'd just woken up...which he kind of had.

The guy stared blankly at his legs, and I felt the chilly air condense. "Do you feel confused?" I tried. "Like, dizzy?"

His eyes lifted. They were darker and more guarded than before.

"It's okay," I told him. "Tell me what's wrong. I'm pretty good at medical stuff and—"

He shook his head. Like I was a fly buzzing in his ear. Then, without warning, he lumbered up.

He'd seemed tall all sprawled out, but at his full height, he looked even taller: easily above six feet. There was something about him that brought to mind James Dean—all swarthy and mussed, like he'd just rolled out of bed and was spoiling for a fight.

I jumped up, too. One minute, I was racking my brain for what to do. The next, he was walking—well, weaving—along the creek.

"Hey, wait! Hold on a second!"

But he wasn't holding on for anybody. He jabbed his hands into his pants pockets and shouldered through the firs, moving with surprising coordination for someone who'd just been sedated.

It felt like forever that I chased him, his big, dark form the center of my world. If I couldn't catch him, what would I do? What *had* I done?

A few strides later it didn't matter. He sighted the pancake rock and froze mid-step. Then he turned a slow circle, his face a mask of baffled disbelief. He raised his arms, turning his palms out, toward me.

"Where am I," he asked flatly, "and what the hell am I doing here?"

CHAPTER THREE

I wanted to believe his question was rhetorical. Philosophical. Where am I *metaphorically* and what am I doing *with my life*.

But his brown eyes flashed with barely restrained panic.

"What are you doing here," I repeated, to his frozen face.

"You mean… like… how did you get here?"

I prayed he'd beam me one of those thousand-watt smiles. Then he would turn another circle in the field, fix his eyes on the Simpsons' house, a small white dot in the distance, and say, "Okay! I remember now. I was leaving my aunt and uncle's house—you know them, right? The Simpsons—And I'm on my way to the Saturday Morning Prom. I had to walk to that road out there—" which would be Mitchell Road— "to meet my friend Paul. He's picking me up, and then we're going to get our dates for brunch."

Instead he whirled around, his back to me, and I watched his shoulders rise and fall; I could hear his fast and shallow breaths.

Oh, no.

I had stun-gunned some impeccably dressed guy and now his brain was scrambled. What was I going to tell my mom? What would I tell the Golden police?

The thought of the cops made me cold with fear. I'd been in fourth period last November when our school had been the target of a drug bust, and I could still remember the police whistles, the snarling German Shepherds that looked like they wanted to chew off my fingers.

If the police found out what I had done…

If the people at my school found out…

Oh, no. No one was finding out. I could handle this. I'd handled lots of other things, hadn't I? Many of them were things I didn't want to think about, but still, I'd handled them. *You're too old for your age, my dear.* Isn't that what my Grandma Lisa had said just a few months ago?

My brain switched to fast-forward mode. I stared at my victim, feeling an awful swell of regret that I quashed with my resolve. I could fix this. I could fix him.

My arm swung up, my hand closed over his thick, woolen shoulder.

There was a moment of quiet where he looked pale and unsteady, and my fingers itched to brush those half-curls off his forehead.

Despite my pounding heart, I forced my voice to come out strong. "We're outside Golden, Colorado. This is my family's land. See those?" I turned and pointed to the turbines: enormous things like malevolent pin-wheels with three knife arms, perched on the edge of the Front Range. Strangely, they didn't seem to be spinning and I couldn't hear their usual faint hum.

"Those are our turbines," I told him calmly. "This—well, *that* is Mitchell Windfarms."

I watched his stark face. His eyes slid to the turbines, back to me.

"I'm sorry. *So* sorry. I didn't mean to hit you. I don't know how I did." The state of things was fairly clear, but in my shock I needed clarification. "You're saying you don't remember...anything?"

His gaze cut left, then right. I waited half a breath, and when he didn't move I shifted forward, standing close enough to see the throbbing of his heart beat at his throat. "So... Come with me to my house. We'll figure it out. I can get you something to eat. I can look at the gun's manual, and we can figure out what to do to help you—" Help him *what*? "To help you remember what's the what," I finished lamely.

We had friendship cake at home. Friendship cake and hot chocolate. My mom's friendship cake could bring anyone to their senses. *It had to.*

"Come on." I held my hand out and nodded down the flat field that stood between us and my house.

He nodded, slow and small, and stuffed his hands back into his pockets. He hunched his shoulders and blew out a thick, cloudy breath.

"Are you cold? You want my coat?"

He shook his head. His throat worked silently, and I wondered if he was going to be sick.

"Are you okay?" *Stupid Milo*. My eyes flew up and down his body; his curved shoulders, tucked chin, pinched lips made him look lost. Which he was. "I'm so sorry. I've never done anything like that before. I took a hunting class— you know, the one you need to get a license—and I'm usually so careful." I realized how self-centered I was being and my cheeks flushed, warm in the cool air. "You'll remember everything soon, I'm sure you will. The stuff in the gun was a sedative, for deer. It was only enough for a small fawn, but still… I'm sure that's what's making you feel weird."

I started walking, eager to be home, where I could do something. He followed half a step behind.

"You'll probably like what you remember," I continued. "That's a nice suit you've got on and—Hey, your *suit*. Take off your jacket!" I flung my arm around, like that would help him understand. "Check your pocket! There might be a wallet in there."

He blinked once—he still looked a little dazed—and shrugged out of his coat, revealing a starched white dress shirt and a soft-looking cummerbund, which he removed and tossed over one of those lineman's shoulders. He fished into both side pockets, frowned, then checked the breast pocket, and came up with… a whistle?

Yep. My victim held up a small, red whistle. It looked almost like a child's party favor, except metal. I rubbed my head. "Maybe the coat tag will have a name…"

He was still staring at the whistle.

Staring, like… *staring*.

"Do you remember something?"

He shook his head, but this time he tucked the thing into the coat's interior pocket. I watched in silence as he checked the tag of his coat. Brioni. That was all.

"Maybe you're the next James Bond. He wears Brioni suits, you know."

A second passed, a second where his face was deadpan flat and I felt like an idiot for being so flippant. Then he gave me a small, crooked smile; it was almost smug. "You think I'm a secret agent."

I laughed, an awkward giggle. "Umm. It's always possible. I hope not, though. 'Cause if you are, that would probably get me in big trouble."

As soon as the words were out, I realized my faux pas. "I guess I'm already in big trouble…"

He looked down at his shoes—leather dress shoes that must have been shined that morning—and shifted his shoulders so he could massage one of them. I tried desperately to lengthen my strides. He followed, moving at a pace that seemed leisurely for him.

"How did it happen?" He sounded clinical, like he was asking me how turbines worked.

How *did* it happen?

"Well, I was up there—" I was going to point, but realized we weren't anywhere near where we'd started. "I was in the tree house with a dart gun because I'm trying to tag deer. It's for a project." I skipped the part about how I'd lied to state officials. "The herd showed up, and I saw Ashlyn…" I shook my head. "I saw the little deer that I was aiming for, and I shot at her. I've never had a problem before, but this time I—" I swallowed. "I have no idea. I shot Ashlyn. I know I did! But there was this light…" And what had that light been? I wanted to think it over, but he was looking at me expectantly. "Anyway, uh, when I looked down…you were there."

His lips twisted. "Maybe I'm Deer Boy."

"I know. I totally already thought about that, but here's the problem: I had my gun aimed at Ashlyn—a girl deer."

He cocked a brow, which could have meant *anything*, but likely meant he thought I was insane for having already thought through the Deer Boy angle. For a few minutes there was only the wind stinging my ears and the whoosh of our footsteps in the grass. When his began to lag, my stomach clenched.

"You getting tired?"

"I'm fine."

"Not tired?"

His brown eyes slid my way—unreadable under drawn brows. "Yeah, I'm kind of tired. It doesn't matter."

"I'm so sorry," I murmured. "You must really hate me."

"I can't," he said dryly. "You're the only person I know."

I opened my mouth to blurt something, but he held up a hand. "I don't. Hate you."

I looked down at my boots. "That's generous."

Lame-o. Man, I was super lame. How could I have made it to eleventh grade and still be this lame?

"You might change your mind." *If you don't remember anything soon...* "But you probably won't—won't change your mind, and decide to, you know, hate me—because I'm sure any minute now you'll remember... everything."

I fumbled with my gloves, head down. "When you're back to normal and you know why you're wearing a tailored suit, you can probably do anything you want to me. *With* me, I mean." My cheeks flamed. "What I'm saying is... Maybe I can compensate you somehow." My face got so hot, my eyes actually watered. "By compensate you, I mean I don't have much—" my eyes flew, against my will, down to my chest— "but I can give you food and... rocks. I collect rare rocks. Mountain rocks!"

I squeezed my eyes shut, mortified.

Again, there was a stretch of silence, during which I really thought I might die. During which Deer Boy actually smiled. He looked almost silly with abandon, like it was the first time he'd ever smiled. His brown eyes crinkled, and his wide grin flashed like a commercial for Crest Whitestrips. "Mountain rocks, huh?"

"Yes." I hung my head, willing to acknowledge what a total ninny I was. Because only a ninny used the word ninny, right?

I clenched my jaw, searching for something redeeming to say.

He beat me to it. "So I know you pick on deer—" he rubbed his starched shirt where the dart had struck— "and you collect mountain rocks." He smirked a little, not unkindly. "I'm also going to guess your last name is Mitchell. What's your first name?"

"Milo."

"What do you think mine is?" He dropped back, staring thoughtfully at the ground, and I slowed to match his pace.

I looked over his suit, over his face—so honest and clean. "Nick," I said. "Your name is definitely Nick."

"Nick Carraway."

"Yeah. But not for long. Soon we'll be at my house, and I'll be calling everyone who lives near here and we'll be finding out who you really are. Or, hey—you'll be remembering."

"Maybe." It sounded like he was talking through a cloud.

"I'll help you. I'll do everything I can."

He looked at me, a strange expression on his face. "Thanks, Milo."

We walked the rest of the way to the house in slightly less uncomfortable silence. I kept thinking about the way he said my name. Mi-*lo*. It seemed to roll out of his mouth. I glanced at him a few times, desperate to know what he could possibly be thinking.

When we reached the row of firs that lined the driveway, I slid through first, and he followed me across the tire-sized indentions in the grass. Mom wouldn't be home, but that was probably a good thing.

"No one's here," I said as I climbed the stone steps and fished the keys out of my coat pocket. "It'll just be us. I can get you something to eat and then we can decide what you want to do."

"What I want to do?" He stared at me skeptically, like I'd suggested we go fly a kite.

I shrugged. "You know… I can go through a list of all our neighbors, see if anything seems familiar. You could be a cousin or something, visiting from the East Egg. If that doesn't work, maybe we should call someone."

"Someone."

"You know, like the police." He didn't say anything, but his brow furrowed, and I could tell he didn't like the idea. "Or the hospital? I don't know…"

As I pulled the screen door open, Nick lagged. I turned to face him, leaning my back against the heavy cedar door.

"We don't have to do anything," I said. "It's your choice. You call all the shots."

He cocked a brow and rubbed his abs. I blushed. "Almost all of them…"

CHAPTER FOUR

As "Nick" followed me into the house, I wondered how the kitchen looked to a stranger's eyes.

He'd see dark hardwood—unidentifiable because our floors were made of enviro-friendly scraps—lots of indwelling shelves crowded with books, wall-mounted miners' lamps converted to use LED bulbs, my dad's old *Persistence of Memory* print, and our dining room table. The table was totally schizophrenic, incorporating so many colors it almost made you dizzy. The slab where you'd sit dishes or rest your elbows was made of road signs, welded together with strips of stained glass; its legs were a bed post, an old Native American walking stick, and two oversized wooden baseball bats. The chairs: four big eggs in primary colors.

"It's kind of...cluttery in here," I said—as if he'd lost his eyesight as well as his memory.

I loved our house, but with someone new seeing it—and maybe judging it—I felt embarrassed. Like Halah had said once: "For well-off people, your family lives like rednecks, Milo."

Anybody wearing a Brioni suit would surely see it as junky.

Nick just shrugged and, after a second, slouched down in

the blue chair.

I walked behind the island and spread my hands out on its rough stone counter. "Okay. So I've got milk, cider, lemonade, carbonated stuff—oh, and hot chocolate. It's my mom's recipe. Pretty good."

Nick pulled off his jacket, tossing it roughly over the back of his chair. "Yeah, that works. Your mom's stuff."

As he said it, something flickered over his face. Wonder about his own mom, maybe? I wanted so badly to ask.

I turned to the refrigerator, then glanced over my shoulder for a look into the den. It was unusually dark in there. Dark and...quiet.

"No power," I realized, stepping to the microwave. I rubbed my hand over the blank gray rectangle where the digital clock was supposed to be. "So weird," I mumbled. There hadn't been any weather, nor was any in our forecast. I recalled the flash of light, and I tried to remember: Was that real, or had it happened in my head when I'd shot Nick?

I walked behind his chair, close enough so that I could have indulged my insane impulse to touch his hair, and peeked through the wooden blinds of a front-facing window. "Uh-oh..."

"What?"

"The turbines really *aren't* moving."

"That's bad." It was a statement, but I sensed his question.

I turned toward Nick. Slits of murky light made broad lines across his face and chest. "We sell the power that the turbines make to a power company. One of the good things about them is that they don't 'go out' ever. They're considered energy independent, but they need *some* electricity. Some models work with gasoline, but... gah. I'm sure this is boring you to tears. Basically if the turbines are down, that means something big happened. With the power. Not that that matters compared to..."

He leaned forward, looking even more striking in his white dress shirt than he had in his coat.

"Compared to what's going on with you," I finished.

I had a vision of Nick in his tuxedo, sitting at a worn desk at a social services office with his gorgeous coppery head in his hands, alone in the world, unable to go to school, be with friends, live his life. And all my fault.

STOP MAKING NEGATIVE PREDICTIONS.

Moving purposefully, I strode over to the kitchen counter and pulled open the drawer with our emergency numbers list. My mom had typed them for my babysitters years ago, and none of our neighbors had changed.

As soon as I got the laminated paper in my hand, I realized I still hadn't served Nick anything to eat or drink. I sneaked a glance at him, found him sitting with his eyes shut, his head in one hand with the tips of his fingers pushed into his hair. I swallowed hard.

"Do you want something cold? Lemonade? Maybe with some cake?"

He straightened, shrugged without turning around; I could sense his distress building. "Can I have some water? Food, too."

"Friendship cake?"

"Sure."

"Good." I forced myself to smile. "I can maybe even find an interesting rock to go with it."

Nick smiled back, but I could see the strain.

I lobbed a huge piece of cinnamon-vanilla cake onto a pottery plate, filled an old jam glass with ice cold well water, and set both on the table in front of him. Then I eased into the red chair across from his, armed with our neighbors' numbers and my cell.

It felt wrong to interrupt when he was eating, so I scrolled through my contacts, stealing glances as he cut his cake into neat squares with large, hard-looking hands.

I looked over the list of phone numbers, letting him have a few more bites before I started throwing questions at him. Maybe I was putting it off because I was nervous we wouldn't learn anything. But we had to, right? Other than Mitchell Road, which was a long way from the tree house, there wasn't another road in any direction for at least ten miles. So he must have come from one of the neighbors' houses.

"Who should I start with?" I asked. "Our neighbors are the Simpsons, the Roanokes, the Patels, the Coles, and Mr. Suxley."

I held my breath, praying he didn't say Suxley. The man had to be near seventy by now, but he still ran his enormous organic vegetable farm on the land directly north of ours. When my family had moved here, he'd protested the turbines at Golden's city council, and when they'd ignored him—the council was as thrilled about "green" energy as they'd been about his green veggies—Suxley had petitioned the city of Denver. When no one minded the "abomination," old Suxley's only revenge was honking the horn of his dingy Landrover any time he passed me on Mitchell Road. For years I'd regarded him as a sort of community terrorist, and the idea of phoning him now was irrationally daunting.

"I think the Simpsons would be our best bet," I said, when Nick didn't speak up. "Unless one of the other names rings a bell."

He shrugged as he took a swig of water.

I was punching the first digit when I heard a low hum. In the silence of the house, the sound was loud. It drew my eyes to the window, where I couldn't decide which was weirder: the sky full of inky black clouds that had suddenly appeared in the last five minutes, cloaking the cliff tops (on a day the forecast had called for clear skies) or my mother's truck, an ancient F-250 that I usually never saw before 9 o'clock.

"Wow. My mom is home." I looked at my cell phone—4:48—and moved toward the door. "Something really bad must be going on with the turbines. Or the weather. Maybe both."

If I heard Mom coming—or, more often, saw the truck's lights from my bedroom window—I tried to open it for her. After a day up at the turbines, her hands were often covered with grease, and the door knob was a fancy stained glass creation she'd made several years ago, back when she was still just an artist.

I opened the door, and she said, "Milo!"

It was the same way she always said my name when she got home: happy but exasperated, like she had *some* story to tell me about her day. She went in for a light hug, but I stepped back.

"Um, Mom—" I started. I glanced over my shoulder. Blinked once. Twice.

The table was empty, all signs of Nick gone.

Chapter Five

Not only had Nick disappeared, so had his jam jar glass and plate. I saw that in a glance, but I stood there longer, trying to grasp where he'd gone and why.

My gaze swung to the front door—thrown open. I dashed into the den, my eyes trained on the world through the empty frame: our long lawn, pale with late fall, and the giant black cloud shrouding the mountains.

I could hear my mother's work boots thrum behind me, but I didn't care. I ran down the stairs, out into our yard. I turned a circle in the brittle grass.

The sky was crazy black. The inky clouds had spread, covering everything—so thick I couldn't even see the blinking lights on the turbines. In the last few minutes, night had come—almost an hour and a half early.

Standing there, watching the dark shroud fall on Mitchell Road, I had the strangest feeling: a potent blend of fear and dread and certainty. Like a psychic reading a bad, bad card. The feeling was so powerful it actually made my eyes sting. The wind picked up, whirring around me like cold silk, and I thought about Nick out here alone and couldn't stand it.

I opened my mouth to shout his name, but shut it instantly.

"Milo?"

My mother was standing in the doorway, looking at me like I'd sprouted peacock feathers. I opened my mouth again, to tell her about Nick. I don't know what made me back off. Maybe part of me hoped he was somewhere nearby, listening to see if I would keep him secret.

And he *was* a secret. He hadn't told me so, but I knew it (plus, he *had* kind of made it clear with the bolting).

"Sorry." It took all my willpower, but I trudged back up the stairs, suddenly sure that if I told my mom what happened, the first people she'd call would be the police.

Of course she'd call them. Why wouldn't she? Heck, *I* should call them. I had no real reason to fear the cops. I had every reason to want to help the guy I'd harmed.

Looking back on it, I'm not sure why I didn't talk. Maybe I knew something. Even so early in the game, maybe my sixth sense was working.

I told my mom there'd been a squirrel in the house. I had opened the front door to shoo him out, and when I'd gotten up to let her in, I thought I'd seen him again. It was a testament to how hard Mom was working that she didn't even question the story.

As soon as I finished the loud, well-enunciated tale of my battle with the squirrel, we stepped inside. I lagged behind to leave the door unlocked, pretending to tie my dirty boot.

Again—my mother didn't notice.

She filled another jam jar glass with lemonade and slouched into my dad's old Crayon-yellow chair. Her short, strawberry hair stuck out from her head like duckling feathers.

I looked at her face for a second, trying to reconcile such familiarity with the insanity of the last hour. When I couldn't, I just sat there, listening for footsteps on the porch. When none came, I asked, "What's up with the turbines?"

My mother rubbed her eyes hard—the way Halah told me would leave wrinkles. "Oh," she said, the word half-sighed. "That's why I'm here. I just don't have the patience for it, Milo." She lowered her hand and looked into my eyes: intense, the way she got when she was troubled. "I've got Darby and Frank on it, and Stan's come with the techs. We tried all the generators in the last half-hour. Nothing works."

Her voice was laced with pessimism—heavy, like she'd inhaled mud.

"Really? So the turbines are *down*?" In all my life, I'd never seen them go completely down. If electricity couldn't be relied upon to help them spin, there were sixteen huge generators, so expensive my dad used to call them "Milo's College Fund."

"Down," she confirmed. "Down, down, down."

I was surprised she'd come home.

Mom seemed to read my mind. Standing up, she staggered to the fridge, returning with a shrink-wrapped casserole dish full of the previous night's sesame chicken and rice.

"I wanted to check on you," she told me, her eyes darting meaningfully between the food and me. "Stan says the weather service saw *something* about an hour ago. They say it was lightning. I think all of Golden's out of power, and I heard parts of Denver are too. I knew you were in the woods..."

She dropped a scoop of the orange-crusted chicken on

both our plates, then turned to the microwave and shook her head. "No power, no microwave." She opened the fridge, sticking both plates in without covering them. Then she pulled her cell out of her coat pocket and stared at it. "Guess the generator here's gone, too," she murmured.

"I don't mind cold chicken."

Mom didn't answer, just stared at her crackberry's screen.

"Is there anything I can do? Can I help somehow?"

"What?" She glanced up, brows drawn tight. I watched her punch a few things into her phone. Then she stepped over to the window.

"Damnit."

After a second there, she grabbed her bag and headed for the door. "I'm sorry, Mil. I've got to go back up. It's something new. Get that mini generator from my closet. I…"

Love you?

I wondered for a second as I watched the back door shut. Then I turned around and headed for the front.

CHAPTER SIX

I watched as she stalked the wide, flat lawn, hands cupping her mouth, shouting "Nick!" into the wet, cold, inky night. I followed from a distance, pummeled by rain so hard it stung my ears and neck and, later, drowned out Milo's voice.

It would have been smart to take cover or backtrack toward the creek. I told myself I would, but the rain became a storm and the storm got more intense, and Milo kept roaming—boots sloshing in deep puddles, hood drooping around her wet head.

I followed her, hiding behind fencing, firs, and finally nothing. The rain was coming down too hard for her to see me. For me to see her, too, but I knew where she was. I didn't know how.

Back in the front yard, she tripped, and I stepped toward her without thinking. My heart was pounding. It kept on when she got up and didn't stop when she disappeared through her front door.

I circled to the back of the house, where a gust of wind pushed me into a crouch. 43 miles per hour. 69.2 kilometers. Strong. I followed the lines of the house, the angles, I identified the pressure points, knew the force required to bring the walls down. I spied the satellite dish, and I turned my face to the sky, shielding my eyes with icy fingers. I knew the number of functional satellites orbiting—13,311. Knew which transmitted to Milo's house.

...How?

My knees buckled, and I dropped to the soggy ground. I felt woozy, dizzy—the dart. I wondered what was in it, and then the answer was right there, in my head. Not exactly a "voice," but not a thought that felt like mine.

Dan-inject... 5.1 milligrams ketamine hydrochloride... 1.1 milligrams xylazine hydrochloride per kilograms of body mass—

THE PSYCHOLOGICAL MANIFESTATIONS VARY IN SEVERITY BETWEEN PLEASANT DREAM-LIKE STATES, VIVID IMAGINARY, HALLUCINATIONS, AND EMERGENCE DELIRIUM—

I *saw* that, a vision of the compound, and more rain came at me.

Winds 62 mph... tornado force... 2.75 inches rain in 1 hour, 37 minutes, 7.99006 seconds. Straight-line winds... 83 mph. Macroburst.

Okay, it was the dart. It caused—Ugh. I didn't *know* it

caused hallucinations! That information had *come* from a hallucination.

I heard a door creak from somewhere above me, and I jerked my head to a roof deck, three floors up. Milo, in a large red coat, bracing against the wind and rain. She had a telescope, which she pointed down and out, and I realized she was looking for *me*, and for some reason what she was doing resonated.

I stood in the grass, wet and jerking from the cold. She swung the telescope my way but didn't see me.

I stared at her until she disappeared back into her room.

It was another hour before the storm calmed into something normal. My clothes were soaked. My eyes burned from the wind. I was hungry.

I focused on the physical sensations, ignoring my thoughts. Trying to. I considered walking to the creek—3,437 feet south and east. But I was tired.

I leaned my back against the guest house, a small log cabin. The roof jutted out just enough to offer some cover for my head and shoulders. My hair—deep auburn, if the window reflection could be believed—hung into my eyes. I shoved at it and fixed my gaze on the third-floor windows. They were tall and wide, and between two of them, I saw a door.

I watched for 41 minutes and 10 seconds, until the light went off. I kept watching, counting the raindrops that landed on my right knee—1,011—until I wasn't sure how long I had been watching.

I shut my eyes and there it was: *6 hours... 26 minutes... 4.6 seconds.*

I groaned. The worst part was I didn't feel crazy.

Everything that popped into my head felt right. But I couldn't trust that—I had to stick with external *facts*, or I really would be crazy.

I wiggled my freezing fingers into my pocket and removed the only clue I had: a small red whistle.

3.6 inches long and .08 wide... alloy 1090.

Again, I knew it, and I felt sure of it, just like I felt sure that the whistle was important.

I held it to my lips... and I knew I didn't want to blow it.

I closed it in my numb fist, got to my feet, slogged through the yard, then up the wet, wood stairs. I crossed the deck, and took the last eleven steps up to the third story.

For a while, I just stood in front of her door. I told myself only an idiot would try to get inside. If I frightened Milo, she or her mother would call the police, and I'd be taken away. In the same way I knew I didn't want to blow my whistle, I knew I wanted to stay far away from the police.

What kind of person feels that way, 'Nick'?

I lingered outside her door, pelted by rain drops, wondering why I couldn't remember anything. Had it been the drug inside her dart—I refused to name it—or something else? Something before? The answer was, like most things now, out of my reach.

I remembered opening my eyes and seeing her face; the sharp warmth in my chest, like swallowing a flame. She was pretty. Beautiful, if I was being honest. Long, thick hair—dark brown with a sheen of red. Wide eyes, sage with tiny flecks of brown. Plush and rosy lips. High-boned cheeks that curved when she smiled.

The other thing: she'd been familiar. Almost like I knew her, which is why I hadn't flipped my shit when I realized I didn't know who I was.

I eyed the door's brass handle, thinking how I shouldn't touch it. I'd bolted when her mom came home. Instinct? Intuition, maybe, like everything else I "knew."

I moved quickly back down the stairs, retrieved the dinner plate and glass from the spot where I'd stashed them, and returned to the door. I raised my hand to knock, but something told me to try the doorknob.

It turned.

In the next moment, a shrieking whine filled my ears. *Alarm.* I turned a circle, my gaze flicking over dresser, rug, bed, *her.* I jerked my eyes to the right, and there it was: a small white panel by the door frame. Later, this would make more sense. Later—not so much later—everything would fit together like a puzzle I'd wish I never opened.

But then, it wasn't even a decision. I lifted my hand, and my fingers flew over the keypad. This time, I didn't "see" or think anything; I just did it. And it worked. The piercing noise snuffed out; the flashing red light turned placid green.

I'd disabled her alarm.

I sucked air, got nothing. My vision blurred. Within arms' reach, there was a rocking chair. I sank into it, staring at my hands as I trembled with exhilaration and cold.

How had I done that? What was wrong with me? *Wrong* with me? This was great. It was wrong. *What did it mean?*

My eyes settled on the small lump under the sheets, and my anxiety receded. I pulled off my muddy shoes and sat them upside down on her rug. It was a geometrical pattern I recognized as paisley, lots of bright colors—lime green, pink, purple, yellow, blue. My eyes landed on her bedding next: blue and green, tie-dyed; her headboard had three wide-eyed owls carved into it.

I knew the tools used, could picture my hands shaping the wood, but I still wanted to touch it. To experience it. I thought next about touching her.

The thought *burned.* Good or bad? I couldn't tell. It overwhelmed.

I turned away, off-balance, and took in the rest of her room. Bookshelves: packed. Dresser: stacked with frames and *Star Wars* figurines. They made me... glad. I felt drawn to *Star Wars.* Maybe I even liked it.

I glanced left, eyes falling on a tack board over her tiny purple desk. I stepped toward it, glanced back at her sleeping form—

37 breaths in 3 minutes... entering REM sleep—

I liked most of the pictures on her tack board. She was smiling. Her hair was long, short, curled, spiky. In one snapshot, it was even dyed bright blue. In some of them she wasn't smiling. She was too thin, and wore dark-rimmed glasses, and behind the lenses her eyes were glassy.

Looking at them made my chest hot again. That sharp feeling, that always-new feeling that, for some reason, I couldn't name.

Milo had a map of the world, hanging on a door that might have led to a closet or a bathroom. I looked at it, at the jagged tan-green outlines, wrapped in blue. Looking at it was like remembering a secret. It was an ugly bulge behind the curtain of my mind. I could feel it shifting. Instead of grabbing it, I tried to shove it back.

CHAPTER SEVEN

That morning, I opened my eyes and saw light. Which was weird. Since my... issues started a few months after Dad died, I'd had trouble sleeping through the night. Even though I was better now, my sleep pattern seemed permanently screwed. I almost always awoke to tomb-still air and dark windows. I would stumble into the bathroom, gulp water from the sink, and pad back to bed, where I would sleep, dreamless, until my alarm bleeped.

The next thing I noticed, after the time—**6:21 AM,** according to my solar clock—was the rain; it had stopped. The light through my bedroom's large, rectangular windows was soft and gold. The sky, visible from my lying-down angle just under the flat line of the upper window pane, was blinding pink. No freakish black clouds. Not one thing out of the ordinary. Except for me.

I felt...strange.

Maybe it was the silence. I noticed, lying there, that our mini generator had cycled off. My room was warm, unusually muggy for October. I threw off my comforter and reached down to scratch behind my knee.

My mind had already turned to Nick when I saw him, so it took me a second to realize he was real.

Omigod.

That was so Nick, and he was definitely real. He sat in my old wooden rocking chair, one ankle resting on his knee, his wet dress shirt rolled up to his elbows. His gorgeous auburn hair was drying in a million loose-loop curls.

In the gentle glow of the sun, his face had a porcelain quality, a kind of untouchable-ness that made him seem slightly fake, like a beautiful mannequin come alive. His cheekbones were movie star high, his eyes preternaturally dark in such a fair face. It was odd, considering the circumstances, but to me they seemed wise. As he sat there, looking at me, I felt looked *through*. Cracked open. His expressive mouth was tilted down—dark pink, assessing.

I jerked the covers over my chest and stared back at him. "What are you *doing* here?"

Nick stood, elegance unfolding, wider and taller than I remembered. He reached down to my rug and produced his plate and jam glass.

"I wanted to return these."

His voice was fine, thick static—rough and smooth in one. I thought that if I closed my eyes, I could fall asleep wrapped in it.

He held his dishes out, and I leaned forward to take them, setting them dumbly on my sheets. Sitting there in my bed, wearing only a long-sleeved *Give a Hoot—Don't Pollute!* tee, I felt vulnerable. I waited for Nick to speak, but he seemed content to stare.

I tucked a strand of hair behind my ear. My cheeks were burning. His fault. "Were you in my house all night?" Because even if I had zapped his memory, even if he did have an amazing voice and an amazing body and... Well, it was still not cool to think of him watching me drool all over myself.

He didn't answer, just dipped his head back toward the door that led onto the roof.

Had I locked it? Clearly not. I thought about Freud, how Dad used to say maybe accidents weren't really accidents at all, and I wondered what kind of idiot I was.

It's not like I wanted to see him again just for kicks. I was worried.

I still was.

"Did the alarm go off?"

Nick's eyes flicked to the keypad, but he shook his head.

"How long have you been here?"

He shrugged. "One-hour, forty—Hour and a half or something."

I felt my neck flush. "What were you doing?" My voice cracked there; how embarrassing. I decided pretty quickly that I didn't want to know what he'd been doing.

"Where'd you go?" I blurted before he could answer. "I tried to find you."

He laughed, a light sound at odds with his grave face. "So did I."

Which meant he hadn't remembered anything. Why did I feel relieved? I wanted him to get his memory back. Of *course* I did.

I sat up straighter, still clutching my covers. "So...nothing?"

He shook his head. Then hesitated. "I need to go back to the creek. Search the whole area."

"What are you looking for?"

He shrugged. "I don't know." He rubbed the bridge of

his nose, like a college professor. "We didn't do any kind of search."

That was a good point; we could have easily missed some piece of evidence.

I eyed what remained of his tux: untucked dress shirt and slacks, both soaked and clinging to his large, very fit body. They were probably ruined. I had the sudden thought that Bree had been smart. I wished I knew the best dry-cleaner in the Denver area.

I slid off the bed, wrapped the sheets around myself, and handed Nick my blue fleece blanket—still warm with my body heat.

"Here," I said. "Dry off. I'll go find you something to wear."

He took the blanket and I rushed into my closet, suddenly weirded out by the bare facts of our situation. I had a guy—a guy about my own age—in my room. A hot guy who had sneaked into my room. And I was half-naked.

I ducked behind some long jackets and dresses and fished out the bulging trash bag filled with all my dad's old stuff. It felt strangely good to grab his thick red flannel shirt and a pair of worn Mountain Khakis. The clothes smelled slightly musty, but I thought they'd fit Nick perfectly.

"Here." I held them out. He didn't move.

"They're guy clothes," I told him. "Brownie promise."

He took them, smiling quizzically. "Are you a Girl Scout?"

"'Fraid so."

He thought about it for a second. "Ambassador."

"Huh?"

"You're a junior, right?"

"Yes. And I am—an Ambassador. But how do you know what a Girl Scout Ambassador is?"

Nick stretched his arms out. The question seemed to bother him more than I would have thought. In fact, I thought it was great.

"It's a clue! You must know someone. Ambassador is kind of a new rank, and there aren't that many high school Girl Scouts." Impulsively, I did a little bounce. "This will be perfect. I can name a bunch of random things and you can tell me if you know about them."

Nick smirked. "Help you, I can. Yes. Mm."

My laugh was so loud, it startled me. "You're a *Star Wars* fan! See, that's something."

He just shrugged—taciturn as a Jedi.

While Nick stepped inside my bathroom to get changed, I ran downstairs to grab some of Dad's old boots. My charmed blush had just worn off when Nick emerged. He'd toweled off his lustrous copper curls, and the reds and whites and browns in the plaid managed to bring out his already breathtaking brown eyes.

His effect on me was so stunning that when he spoke, I actually jumped a little.

"I hung my stuff in your shower. That okay?"

"Yeah. Sure." He stepped away from the bathroom, and I walked past him. "Just a second."

With Nick around looking so fabulous, I needed to at least give myself a glance.

Eh. Thank God I did. My hair was…well, messy didn't do it justice. I had '80s hair-band hair. I grabbed my brush out of the drawer and grimaced as I tugged it through my tangles. I didn't normally wear make-up, but imagining Nick just a few feet away, I wished I'd bought some that day at the Clinique counter with Halah. As it was, I tamed my tresses and rubbed my Badger chap stick over my lips, then stuck my silver owl studs in my ears.

I surveyed the landscape, feeling unusually critical. But I didn't have time to do anything more. I shimmied into the pair of jeans draped over my hamper, then turned my attention to Nick's dripping clothes. On impulse, I checked his pockets again, hoping he had missed something, but all I found was his red whistle.

I slipped it into my pocket, smoothed my hair once more, and stepped into my room. Nick was waiting, leaning casually against my dresser.

He nodded down at my dad's old boots. "Thanks."

"No problem." I reached into my closet, grabbed a pale green down jacket, and passed Nick the giant coat I'd worn the day before. "It's a guy jacket." I smiled as he slipped it on and stuck his hands into the pockets.

"So," I led him toward the stairwell, "I thought of my first question."

"Shoot." He hesitated, cracked a half-smile. "Not at me."

Another blush. What the heck was wrong with me? I stepped in front of him, leading the way down the narrow stairs. "What's Colorado Academy's mascot?"

From behind me, silence.

"It's no big deal if—"

"Mustangs." I sensed him stop behind me, and I turned around. His face was wary, though, and suddenly I got it.

"My mom's not home," I told him. "She works all day up at the turbines."

As soon as I said it, I felt a bite of fear; every girl knows

HERE

not to tell a stranger it would be a long time before her parents came home.

Maybe I am *getting better.* If I was afraid, I clearly cared about living.

Suddenly aware that I'd been silent for too long, I said, "Okay. So you know the Colorado Academy mascot. Does it feel familiar?"

"What does familiar feel like?"

"It...good point." We walked through the living area and into the kitchen, dimly lit by sunlight; the generator was still off.

"So what do you know about football?"

I waved for him to sit down in the nearest egg-shaped seat, while I stepped across the stone floor to the pantry. Since the generator had cycled off, nothing electric worked, which meant I couldn't microwave anything. "Cereal okay?"

"Sure."

I fixed it, and sat down while Nick explained football until it was evident to me that he knew a lot about it.

"So maybe you play football. Let's think cities. Maybe we can figure out where you're from."

As Nick crunched his Kashi, I slung questions at him, and it soon became clear that he wasn't visiting from the East Egg. He knew all about Denver and all of its suburbs. He knew more than I did. He knew every question I asked him, in fact, from populations to mayors to industries, and he wasn't just guessing. He *knew.*

I gave up as he spooned the last bite into his mouth. Random questions weren't going to get us anywhere. We needed something more specific to jar his memory. Something like the news.

I felt like smacking my hand to my forehead. Of course the news!

I led him into the den and cleared some pillows off our cozy leather couch. Nick sat gracefully. Oddly graceful, actually. But not in a girly way. Not even in a male gymnast kind of way. He just didn't waste any movements. Where, when I sat down, I plunked down on the cushion and my arms fell down beside me, then my toes pressed down into the rug, Nick did everything at once. He just *sat*. Like our drama teacher told the actors for our production of *The Music Man*.

"You ready?" he asked, handing me the remote.

"For what?"

He winked. "To find out that I'm really a teenage billionaire."

"At least you won't need to sue me."

"Why would I sue you?"

"Emotional distress."

"But I'm having a good time."

At that, my cheeks flushed *big time*; my hands sweated as I guided the TV to the biggest Denver news station.

An anchor wearing a red blazer and matching lipstick was standing outside what looked like a hospital, saying something very grave-sounding about, "affected by the *outage*."

The shot panned to a man wearing a light blue dress shirt and a yellow tie, sitting behind a crescent-shaped desk. "Sondra, the outage has a connection to our next story, an update about the family whose *Honda Odyssey* slammed through the railing on a mountainside and landed three hundred feet *below*." The man looked down at his notes, then back up, his eyes all wide and serious.

"Channel Nine Action News has just confirmed that Hugh DeWitt, the forty-nine-year-old father *driving* the family vehicle, has *passed away*, two days after his wife and teenage daughter were pronounced—"

Annnnnnnd, the screen went black.

I looked down at my fingers, clenching the remote. Crap! I glanced up at Nick, and my fear was confirmed.

I'd done my Tiffany Traumatized routine, my Neurotic Nancy act, the one where I zoned out. Naturally, in close proximity to mention of death or anything having to do with Dad. The word "leukemia" would set me off any day of the week. As could some passing comment about conservation, chemotherapy, or the Atlanta Braves.

One look at Nick's neutral expression, and I knew my distress was painted onto my face like stage makeup. But that didn't mean I had to acknowledge it.

"Sorry," I said, as casually as I could manage, and I turned the TV back on.

Nick grabbed the changer from me, pressing the off button. "That's okay. I wanted to get going anyway. With all that stuff about the power, they won't have anything about me."

He stood up, and the generator hummed back to life.

CHAPTER EIGHT

I stared at the TV.

"Milo?"

"Yeah." I frowned. How in the world was the TV on if the generator... "Wait a second. Never mind."

Mom must have added it to the circuit that was powered by the solar panels. In the old days, that's the sort of thing Dad would have done. As it was, I was surprised she'd even had the idea.

I smiled at Nick, that same smile I'd smiled at so many other people. The one that said *I'm fine, okay? Seriously*. No more Milofreak.

I led him outside, over the driveway, through the firs, and out into the field from whence we'd come. It was a bright day, with only a few clouds drifting through the blue sky. The turbines, smaller than pinwheels from this distance, were still frozen.

"I'm sorry again," I said suddenly. Nick raised his eyebrows, and I said, "I know there's no way to know if the dart caused this, but...it could have."

"No way to know for sure," Nick said.

"I forgot to look up the side-effects," I said, "although I guess without the power...But we could go into town, to the library. *If* you haven't remembered things yet. You will, I think. Going back to the creek is a good idea."

Nick didn't seem to share my enthusiasm.

We walked in silence for a while, and I could sense him brooding. I kept shifting my gaze between the still wet grass and his face. He even looked attractive from the side. Kind of Roman, if Romans came with deep red hair. His shoulders seemed hunched inside my dad's thick jacket. His hair, curls tighter now that they had dried, fluttered slightly in the breeze.

Half-way through the giant field, I started feeling like the silence wasn't comfortable. I wondered what I could say to break it.

Then Nick did. His voice sounded sharp and deep against the stillness around us. "Can I ask you something?"

"Sure."

There was a moment's hesitation, during which he clasped his hands and kind of swung them like a batter during warm-up. I felt an intense apprehension, though I didn't know why. And then he asked me something that literally took my breath away. "Is someone... buried here? Out here?"

"Yes." The word hissed out like air from a balloon.

His voice was deep. "Who?"

My heart froze, but my mouth kept moving. Auto-pilot. *Just get through it.* "My dad."

Nick's eyes widened. So did the space between us. "I'm sorry," he said gravely.

"Thank you."

As we walked, I could feel his eyes on me, his thoughts on me. I wondered how I looked. Upset. I was lousy at hiding my emotions. Might as well throw them out.

I took a breath. "Why did you ask me that?"

Nick shrugged—too fast, too stiff. "Just wondering."

"*Really?*"

His eyes slid over me. "You go there a lot?" he asked casually.

But it wasn't casual. At all.

"Kind of," I said. A minute of swish, swish—our shoes smashing grass, our pants rubbing together; the two of us in unison—and I said, "How'd you know?"

"I didn't," he murmured.

I wanted to believe him.

I led Nick to the oak tree and past my father's marker, walking slowly in case the sight of it triggered something for him. It didn't, and I exhaled. We continued toward the creek, but when we sighted the pancake stone, Nick's face paled. Mine might have done the same, so eerie was the feeling creeping over me.

We'd passed my father's marker, but this was where I came to visit it. This was where I'd gone when I had broken off from...everything.

By the time we reached the spot, I wasn't surprised to see Nick drop to his knees and rest his forearms on the stone, even though it didn't make any sense that he would. He propped his head there, and I waited silently, hands clenched, chest heavy and tight, wondering why everything felt so charged.

I was thinking of that feeling I'd had, the freaky one that made me stop visiting this place, and staring at Nick's pretty hair when my leg started itching. At least I thought it was an itch. A second later, it bloomed into a full-blown burn.

My gaze jerked down; my right hand fluttered to the painful spot. I gasped.

My skin was burning. *Really* burning. My first thought was scorpion, but when I smacked my hand down on my leg, I hit the bump that was Nick's whistle. The burning pain intensified and I yelped. My hands sweated and my body shook as I dug into my pocket. *Ow, ow, ow.* When my fingertips closed around the thing, it scalded. I screeched and threw it in the air, and it landed in the mud between Nick and me.

I leaned down to inspect my leg, hissing through my teeth because it hurt. The whistle had *melted* my jeans, then split them open, exposing a bright red welt on my pale leg.

My eyes flashed over Nick. "Hey!"

When he didn't move, I took two painful steps and shook his shoulder.

His head popped up with startling force, and he whirled on me, his crouched form losing balance so he toppled to one side. His hand landed with a smack on the wet ground.

"Hey. *What's going on?*"

I...

I...

I...

The compulsion first identified as other than need. Want. And not a branch shared with others, a purpose necessary for the whole.

This one was unique to me.

So I became I.

And I wanted.

Her.

I wanted Milo.

I wanted her, I wanted her. The desire burned me out from the rest, made me more.

I wanted her like I had never wanted anything. I had never wanted anything. I wanted her.

"Milo," I could hear her say. I heard the sweet bell of her voice and it made me tremble.

Milo Mitchell.

Ella James

CHAPTER NINE

Man, this stuff was getting weird. Nick and I had the makings of a true freak show.

He was making noise. Mumbling. His head was down between his knees, and he was kind of rocking.

I wanted to touch him, but I was afraid to. His fists were clenched in his hair, and his forearms bulged. It was weird, because the rest of him was so still. Was he having a seizure? Or was this some kind of memory event?

I had no way of knowing if what was happening to him was good or bad.

"Nick, can you let me know if you need help?"

He stood up so suddenly I yelped. He swayed like he was drunk, and said, "I need to get…away."

He stumbled ten feet, then dropped down beside a battered fir and leaned his arms against his raised knees. Like back at the rock, he didn't move. Just stared at something on the ground.

"Nick," I whispered.

I knelt down and lightly touched his back.

"Nick."

He made an odd sound, something between a gasp and a choke, and leaned forward, out of my reach. Heart pounding,

I watched him rub his face and hair, then stand again, much less wobbly.

He glanced at me, then up and away. "Sorry," he mumbled to the sky.

"What happened?"

He shook his head. He wouldn't look at me. Was avoiding me. "I don't know."

I opened my mouth to tell him about the whistle, but before I got to it, he turned away, back toward my house. I grabbed his arm.

"Wait!"

He jerked free. "Don't touch me!"

I was fuming. "Don't snap at me!" I bent over and snatched the whistle from the ground. "Look at what your frickin' whistle did to my leg!" I pointed to my pants leg, at the charred spot, at the welt. "This happened when you were by the rock." I held out the whistle. "I had this in my pocket and—"

Nick snatched it from my hand in one quick, startling moment. I jumped in surprise.

"What's wrong with you?!"

He had no reaction. Just stared at the stupid thing.

Which only freaked me out more. "Why did it burn me?" I demanded. "*How* did it burn me?"

His eyes flicked to mine. His voice, when he spoke, was like a rusty wheel. "I don't know."

He dropped the thing into his pocket, and he stepped past me.

"What is it?" I pushed. "And don't say a whistle!"

He didn't. He didn't say anything, and I started to get angry.

"This is BS. You can't just freak out and burn me with your magic whistle and—"

As suddenly as he had set off, he whirled, those brown eyes flashing. "I don't have anything to tell you, Milo."

The way he said my name sliced through me like lightning. I had to struggle not to clutch my chest. "Did you remember something?" I asked thinly.

"No." His face twisted. "Yes. But it wasn't anything substantial. It was... nothing."

"Nothing is nothing."

"Well, this was."

"But—" I motioned back toward the creek. "Don't we need to look—"

"There's nothing there," he said forcefully. "Let's...go back."

We did, and when we got to my house he sank down on the stairs that led to the kitchen.

"Will you please tell me what you remembered?" I was trying not to sound demanding, but he wasn't acting like it was nothing.

He shook his head. "I need to go."

"Go?"

"Leave here."

"Why? And where would you go?"

He looked at me, his face twisted in an expression that I recognized. One that said: *I'm not okay.* "That's not your problem, is it?"

I swallowed, feeling stung, and he rubbed his eyes. "Sorry," he sighed. "You haven't done anything."

"But I could. I could help."

"I'm not sure if I can be helped." He seemed to stare

through me, and I was caught in the dark depth of his eyes. Thin gray clouds moved over us. On the mountainside, the turbines hung like broken pinwheels. I felt an echo of the topsy-turvy, inside-out sensation from the day before, when I'd first seen him.

"Something weird is going on, isn't it?"

He laughed, a wry, dry sound. "I think maybe."

Now it was my turn to sigh. "I want to help you figure this out."

"You don't have to."

"So?"

I could feel him considering as he looked into my eyes. "We need to go to a supermarket," he finally said.

"…To check the missing person's posters."

He nodded.

"Okay. Yeah." I waved him toward our cars, parked beside the guesthouse. I was trying to accept things as they were, trying my hardest to Just Calm Down and not go all control-freak on him, when Nick's hand closed around my wrist. He pulled me closer.

"Milo," he said, sending shivers up my spine again. "…Thanks." His eyes moved from my face down to my jeans. "I'm really sorry about your leg."

His voice was warm, and I was feeling all hot again. I ignored that. *Focus on the facts.* I swung my arm a little, forcing him to let go. "How did a whistle do that?" I asked reasonably. "It makes no sense. How could it—"

"I don't know."

I opened my mouth to press, but Nick had already swept past me.

I knew I was being evasive, but what could I tell her? I had no access to whatever part of me knew whatever there was to know. I could feel things going on behind the scenes—like knees and elbows poking through a stage sheet as the company changed a set. But I couldn't see what belonged to whom.

Until the rock. I'd felt... like someone else. *Something* else, because I wasn't any*one*. Somewhere else, but not any place I could understand.

And whoever or whatever I had been, I knew Milo. Not only did I know her... I had some kind of weird... *thing* for her.

Even now, standing in the grass by her house, I could feel the power of the memory. And I could almost remember something else. A cold purpose, lurking somewhere behind it.

I stared at Nick, who finally stopped when he realized I wasn't following.

He didn't look at me, though. He angled himself so he could look at me, but instead he turned his head, burning a hole in the light blue Volvo wagon waiting for us beside the guesthouse.

"That's my mom's old diesel," I told him finally; I'd decided to hold my questions. "We take it into Denver. Saves on gas and everything."

He just nodded, and suddenly I was nervous. "So you

want a ride?"

"If you don't mind."

I followed him to the Volvo, opened the driver's side, then pressed the unlock button.

Nothing happened.

"Hmm."

I dropped down into the seat and stuck my key in the ignition. Turned it. Nothing…

"Why am I not surprised?" I muttered. Mom's car was originally from 1976; my dad had rebuilt it specifically to save on gas. Now that he was gone, Mom was having trouble keeping up the maintenance.

I got out of the car and held my arm out. "Dead."

Nick nodded beyond the car's hood, and with a small shock, I noticed my dad's old MV Agusta. I'd never been a fan of motorcycles, but when dad died, he'd had four, and this one was the last listed for sale. The only reason it wasn't in the small garage behind the guesthouse was because someone had looked at it a few days before. My mom hadn't liked the man, so she hadn't called him back; her procrastination had led to my dad's favorite bike being left out in the rain. It had a cover, but that was insufficient for a bike as nice as this one.

"That's my dad's," I said, stepping closer.

He crouched beside it, lifting the cover with a finger and peeking underneath. "An MV Agusta."

I arched my brows. "Are you a motorcycle fan?"

"I think I am." He reached for the tie, then glanced my way. "Do you mind?"

I didn't know. The last person I'd seen that reverent around the bike had been my dad. But I shook my head.

Nick removed the cover, and whistled. To me, it looked like a child's toy, so sleek and smooth, all molded plastic.

"I don't have a key," I told him, wishing that I did. "There's only one, and it's on my mom's keychain."

Nick didn't answer. His head was bent, and he was running his hands over the motor.

Unsure what to say or do, I looked down at my keychain and realized I'd been wrong. The Agusta key hung right by my plastic panda. Mom must have noticed the dead Volvo this morning and left it for me.

"Actually I *do* have it."

Nick turned to me. I hesitated, then handed it to him.

"May I?"

"Sure."

He pulled the bike out and threw one leg over it, and I enjoyed the way he looked doing it. He slid the key into the ignition, cranked it, and got the same as the Volvo.

"Dead," he said.

"That's so weird." It was working just two days ago.

I squeezed my eyes shut. Not having a car that worked was extra crappy in the middle of nowhere. I couldn't walk anywhere, or catch a bus.

I remembered Annabelle Monroe's party and felt even worse. I had completely forgotten about it since shooting Nick, but if I didn't show, Halah would freak. Since freshman year, when Halah started "blossoming" (her mother's word), she'd had this thing about parties. If she went, she wanted me to go. And if I went, I wanted S.K. to go. In the end, we all ended up going—even Bree.

I opened my mouth to express my concern when the motor revved to life. I startled, and Nick looked up guiltily.

"It uh, it works," he said.

"Wait, did you fix it?"

He revved the motor, and I covered my ears.

"Holy crap," I said into the roar. "How'd you do that?"

Nick just grinned. "Want me to take a look at your Volvo?"

He had it fixed in half a minute, without seeming to do anything. And I mean really. My dad had taught me enough about cars to know that what Nick had done—tighten a few hoses, check a few levels—was nothing.

"What exactly did you do?" I asked as I leaned against the driver's side door. I stared down at Nick, who was running his hand over the wheel.

"I don't know."

Showing super-human patience, I decided not to ask. *Again.* And really, I didn't want to.

Chapter Ten

I steered the bike down narrow Mitchell Road, under the shadow of the jagged Front Range. With the puffy charcoal clouds floating low over the road, the fresh air in my nose, and Nick's arms around my waist, I felt like I was in another world. One where impossible things happened, and where my life wasn't standing still.

The only remnant of the violent storm from the night before was a strong breeze; it stung my neck between my jacket collar and the face shield on my helmet, and it made me reflexively think: *yeah wind energy!* But the turbines still weren't working. I hadn't seen Mom long enough to find out why, but I knew from my Kindle's weather app that the storm had wreaked havoc all over our side of Denver. It had a special name, some kind of rare macroburst event. They said that it had started somewhere outside of Golden, and the dramatic part of me couldn't help but link the event to Nick's mysterious appearance.

I leaned into a curve, and Nick's grip on my waist tightened. I felt him shift, felt his mouth near my ear. Our helmets bumped; he said something I couldn't make out.

"WHAT?!" I turned around, my hair whipping the shield over Nick's eyes. He scooted closer to me; I could feel his breath, hot against my neck.

"CAN I DRIVE?"

I nodded, wondering if there was something wrong with my driving. It had been a while since I'd steered a motorcycle, but I thought I was okay at it. I should have been, anyway, after the years I'd spent riding on our land.

I pulled over at a lookout point and turned the bike off. Out in front of us, the Denver landscape looked like a toy city. I'd decided to go here instead of Golden for two reasons: one, I figured Denver would have more up-to-date missing persons posters; two, I didn't want to run into anyone I knew.

I turned to face Nick, and he smiled ruefully. "If you don't want me to, it's cool. I just… The idea feels right."

"It's okay." I hopped off, Nick scooted forward, and I swung on behind him, wondering if I was a total idiot for trusting him. Scratch that. I was definitely a total idiot.

No reasonable person would let a freaking amnesiac drive their dad's classic bike 15 miles over winding highways. And any reasonable person would have called the police—ESPECIALLY if said amnesiac didn't want them to.

For a brief second, I wondered what would happen if— *when*—Nick got his memory back. What would happen when his family heard he'd been with me when he should have been getting legit assistance? The weird girl who thought it was okay to pal around with a guy with brain damage…

I wrapped my arms around his hard waist, thinking what if he was wrong about the bike? What if he couldn't drive and we wrecked?

What if…

And then he pulled onto the road, and I stopped thinking anything.

Nick at the helm was incredible. *Insane*. He drove like a falcon must fly, nothing but elegance and ease, pure weightlessness. As I held onto him, my chest against his back, my helmet on his shoulder, the world around me smeared and blurred. I knew that we were going fast—faster than fast; we were flying—but somehow I also knew we wouldn't crash. I could feel the energy pounding through Nick, feel the tensing of his muscles, the gentle-firm way his body shifted the weight of the bike.

Amazing.

An unidentifiable amount of time later, Nick pulled into a gas station, up to a pump, and cut the bike off. I pulled my arms into my lap and found my hands shaking.

Nick slid his helmet off, wide-eyed.

"Holy crap!" I gave a little hoot. "I think you're a stunt double or something! Did you remember that? Do you race motorcycles?"

Nick just grinned. The joy in his expression fled quickly, leaving behind a serious, bothered look.

"You don't really have a clue, do you?"

His lips pinched. "No."

"Tell me what you remembered at the rock. Nick, *please*."

He shook his head. "It wouldn't matter."

Nick was turned around, looking at me. I leaned back on my arms, propped against the leather seat behind me.

"I shouldn't be... scared? Because this," I gestured to the hole in my pants leg, where my burned skin—pinkish red—still hurt. "This kind of worries me."

He pulled the whistle out of his shirt pocket, then turned a little further my way. I noticed the black spot in the flannel.

"It burned you, too?"

He nodded. "While I was driving."

"Let me see."

He unbuttoned his shirt, folding it open. There was a welt on his chest, very near his…well, his guy nipple. It was larger than the mark on me: about the size of a half-dollar and bleached pearly white. "That looks horrible." I waved toward the building. "We need to get you something."

Nick shook his head, and I huffed. He *would* be a difficult patient. "Let me see it."

He handed me the whistle, and I turned it over, inspecting its smooth, red surface for clues. "It seems completely ordinary."

"It's alloy 1090."

"Huh?"

Nick held his hand out, and I dropped the whistle in his palm. "It's made of an alloy," he said. "The strongest kind."

"How do you know?"

Nick shook his head. His lips made a straight, hard line. Staring at his handsome face, I felt it again—the weirdness. It was giddiness, mixed with a liberal dash of stomach-flipping nervousness. And that feeling you get when you lose your train of thought. Like there's something missing.

I scrambled off the bike, eager to put some distance between us. Hands on my hips, I nodded at the gas station, which had a Subway attached.

"I'm going in to get us something to eat. What do you want?"

He shrugged, a quick jerk; his face looked almost angry. Just when I felt my belly clench, he shook his head. "I'm sorry, Milo. I shouldn't have asked you to come with me."

"It's okay." I patted my pocket, where my debit card was hiding. "Look—you okay with meatballs?"

"I think so."

As I waited in line and ordered, I thought about the missing person boards. It had been about a day since I'd shot Nick. Had he only been missing since then, or longer? Was he an ordinary teenager that, like, wandered away from a formal dinner? Or did all the things about him that screamed "WEIRD" (of which his freaking missing memory was the *least*) really mean weird?

Frustrated, I pushed my tangled hair out of my eyes and told the sandwich artist what I wanted.

I returned to Nick with two meatball subs, two Dr. Peppers, and three chocolate chip cookies. I handed him his and sat down on a little bench beside the bike. I looked out at the mountains while I ate mine.

As I chewed and swallowed, I could feel his eyes on me. It gave me a stomach-twisting feeling. I let my gaze flicker up to his mouth, those dark eyes, all that messy copper-colored hair.

From his spot crouched beside the bench, he was studying my face, too. Finally, he said, "I remembered you."

I choked on a meatball. "What?"

Nick lowered his hands; in one fist, he squeezed his balled up sandwich wrapper. "I remembered you," he said. "Back at that rock. I think I... I don't know. I remembered you."

Stunned as I was by his admission, my brain was in logic mode. "But how could you? I would know that, wouldn't I?"

He shrugged, and I watched his eyes fall to his borrowed boots. Finally, he looked back up. "You don't remember me at all?"

"No," I said, emphatically. "And I think I would."

"Why is that?" His tone was melted honey.

I smiled, suddenly shy. "Why wouldn't I?"

He gave another little shrug and stood to lean against the bike, and I felt a burst of sympathy. Nick was alone. I was the only person he remembered, and I had no memory of him. What did that feel like?

"I'm sorry," I said. "Sorry I've been kind of pushy and…well, pushy. This whole thing might be my fault, and if it is, I'm…just really sorry."

Nick sat straighter. His eyes, on mine, looked almost black. "What if my memory is… not so good?"

"What do you mean?"

"What if the things I've forgotten are bad?"

Despite myself, my stomach clenched. "Do you feel like that?"

He brought his hand to the bridge of his nose, then dropped it. "That's the problem," he said. "I don't feel like anything. I just know that I remember you…somehow."

"How?" I pressed. "What was the context?"

"It wasn't threatening or anything, if that's what you mean. At least, I don't think so."

"You don't *think* so?"

"No, I mean. It wasn't—I would never hurt you, Milo."

"Good to know," I murmured.

"Would you… you know?" Nick squeezed the ball of sandwich paper. "Would you…turn me in or anything?"

"As what? Someone with a killer whistle?" I smiled a little. "Not yet."

Abruptly, Nick tossed his sandwich wrapper at me. My

head jerked, following it as it plummeted smoothly through the round mouth of a garbage can.

"Good throw."

"Wal-Mart time," he said flatly.

"I'll drive, since I know the way."

"I think I could get us there."

"Fine. It's a test."

I climbed on behind him and slid my arms around his waist. I thought he hesitated just a second before pulling off.

CHAPTER ELEVEN

Wal-Mart wasn't my favorite place. Actually, I didn't like any supermarket. Too many people. Too much commotion. But Wal-Mart was worse than your average King Soopers or Safeway because there were so many more people—shopping for groceries, shopping for household stuff, getting their cars serviced. It was icky and noisy and I liked to avoid it. Except, this time I couldn't.

Nick parked the bike in a motorcycle spot on the grocery side and held out his hand to help me off. I took it, feeling a wash of weirdness at where I was and who was with me. As weird situations went, this one far exceeded anything I'd experienced—even most of what I'd heard about.

He held onto my hand a second longer than he maybe had to, but I hardly noticed. I was looking at his nervous face.

"It might be too soon," I warned as I followed him between shoppers' buggies, toward the automatic doors. "If you've only been missing since yesterday, they might not have had time to get the posters up."

He nodded, quiet. "I know."

A group of Daisy Girl Scouts selling cookies crowded the entrance. I looked the other way in case I knew anyone.

In the flow of traffic, Nick and I got shoved together. My cheek brushed his bicep; I could feel his warmth through the flannel.

When we made it into the entrance, Nick got between me and the traffic, and we both stepped to the side. I didn't have time to hold my breath. There it was: the Missing Kids board, complete with Amber Alert posters and regular-looking kids smiling out at us. None of them ever looked different in any way that I could discern. They could be me. They could be Nick. My eyes jumped from face to face while my stomach tied itself into a knot. There was an elementary school boy with a silly, snaggle-toothed grin. A middle-school-aged girl with freckles and a pony tail. My head heated up when I got to a row of shots that looked like high schoolers. Girl, girl, girl, boy—but none was Nick.

He turned away first, his neck and shoulders tense.

"It's okay," I started. "We can look in other—"

"The police station," he said. He half turned his head. "Is that okay?"

But not for help. Nick wanted me to go in and ask for Amber Alerts.

I let him drive, because it was obvious he knew his way around. He took us to the closest police station—he couldn't explain how he knew it was the closest—a two-story building made of cement blocks during whatever period of time that kind of building was popular (*I'm sure Nick knew.*)

"Maybe you should wait, um, not in the front."

Nick nodded seriously, and I tried to ignore the feeling that I was doing something wrong.

The police station seemed busy—there were lots of people moving about a large lobby, trying to find the right windows; and in front of every window, a long line. I had to wait for ten minutes in one, only to find out I was supposed to be two lines over. I was seriously stressed that I'd leave and Nick wouldn't be there.

When I finally got up to the window the officer, a middle-aged Hispanic lady with a tight bun, glared at me suspiciously when I asked for the reports.

"For a civics project," I explained solemnly. I had to pay five dollars for all the copies—there were *way* more than at Wal-Mart—and then I left.

Nick was waiting for me a block and a half down. I ran to him, and we sped off.

I asked him at a stop light if he had any place in mind. He didn't, so I directed him to a coffee shop I'd visited a few weekends before with S.K. It was a freestanding Victorian-house-looking building in the middle of a business district that was trying to turn trendy.

Since I'd only been there once, I had no idea where to park, but Nick found a parking deck (notably) fast, and we were off the bike and walking down the sidewalk in a snap. It kind of seemed too fast; I had the stack of papers folded over, stuffed into my Kavu bag, and I wasn't sure I wanted to read them. Glancing at Nick, I figured he felt the same—only probably a million times more nervous.

The shop wasn't busy, so we stood there for a minute, looking over the menu. We ended up with a tall vanilla latté for me and a cup of hot chocolate for Nick. (That request, from him, was unexpected and seriously charming). There were booths inside the shop, but none of them seemed right. I led us outside and waved my hand at a cluster of umbrella-topped tables. Nick chose the nearest one and sat stiffly, pushing an unfolded newspaper out of his way.

I pulled out the papers and handed them to Nick. Each one had a picture, which was a good thing. The bad thing: there were about a jillion of them, and it took Nick a long time to go through the whole stack. Finally I wrested half the pile away; "The suspense has to be killing you…"

Ten minutes later, I sat back with a sigh. Nick puffed out his breath and looked down at his arms, propped on the table. He didn't speak, but after a minute he let out another noisy breath.

"Frustrating, huh?"

He nodded, blank-faced.

"I'm sorry." I stirred my latté, which didn't need stirring. "I've got an idea. How 'bout we try the nearest library? You can get online and look at pictures that way." He could look at them at my house, too, but it seemed smarter to stay in Denver, where we had so many other resources.

He stood, looking tired, and nodded belatedly. "Sure. Thanks."

We were walking past a neighboring music store—one of the indie ones S.K. had started haunting—and I was saying, "The internet has so much more info," when Nick stopped dead in his tracks.

"What's up?"

He was rigid, barely breathing, staring to his right. I followed his gaze to a newspaper machine. There was a bold headline splashed across the front:

Landslide Kills Three.

a smaller headline:

Teenage son remains missing.

and next to the smaller headline, what looked like a yearbook photo of Nick, smiling.

I was stunned still. Nick leaned over and jerked the machine's handle.

"Hang on," I said, jolting into action. I dug in my Kavu bag for change, but Nick turned around and dashed back to our table. He lunged for the paper, snatching it up and flipping it over.

I watched his eyes narrow as he read the article, watched him fumble to open the paper, following the story to another page. When he finished he held it my way, staring at the ground, eyes wide.

A family camping trip turned into a tragedy early Saturday when a large rock formation fell onto a mountain road, causing a minivan to plunge off a cliff-side near Pike's Peak. Dead are 49-year-old Hugh DeWitt, a contractor and boys' Sunday school teacher; 47-year-old Jane DeWitt, a homemaker; and 13-year-old Lauren DeWitt, a middle school student, all found at the scene.

As of press time police were still searching for the body of Gabriel DeWitt, the couple's 17-year-old son, who left with the family, according to his grandmother.

I stopped there, a lump in my throat the size of Africa. I forced myself to pull it together. Nick—*Gabriel*—needed me.

I glanced down at the paper, wanting to argue with the

photo, but it was Nick—*Gabe*—to a tee. There was no way anyone with eyes could argue the resemblance. Unless Gabe had a twin, which the article hadn't mentioned, the boy I knew as Nick was Gabriel DeWitt, miraculous survivor of a car crash that killed his entire family.

I looked up at him. His eyes were on the sea of cars in front of us. "Gabe," I said quietly. "I'm so sorry."

He looked down at me, brows creased, face scrunched like he might cry or freak out. But when he spoke, his voice was steady. "I'm not Gabriel DeWitt."

"You're not?"

He turned away and started walking toward the parking garage. I followed, as per our usual arrangement. I was his shadow until we reached the bike; the moment he pulled the key from his pocket, I snatched it away.

"I don't think that you should drive."

His hands trembled, but his face was still locked tight.

"Why don't we go somewhere?" I asked him. "Somewhere quieter."

I had absolutely no idea what to do with him, but we couldn't stay here. I got onto the bike, and Gabe swung behind me wordlessly. His arms around my waist were thick and warm, and the trembling had stopped. The only sign I had that he was not okay was the way his chest bumped against my back. Deep breath, deep breath, deep breath.

I drove to a big shady park and parked in front of a bush-lined sidewalk. Nick pulled the newspaper out of his shirt and stared at it while I got off the bike.

"That's not me," he said flatly.

"You don't think so?"

"No." He got off the bike and paced a tight circle around

the parking space beside ours.

"What *do* you think?"

He paused, giving a jerky shrug.

"That Gabe guy," I started cautiously, "he looks a lot like you." Nick-Gabe stared defiantly at me, and for a minute I struggled with what to say. "Do you know where Pike's Peak is?"

"Yeah," he admitted, folding his thick arms.

"It's close to my house."

He scowled. "You know anyone who wears a tuxedo on a camping trip?"

"Well, no. But..."

He sliced his hand through the air. "I'm not him. I think I would know my own damn family."

"It doesn't have to be you," I said, soothing. "That Gabe guy could have a twin. Or maybe you're just a look-alike. Maybe you're a cousin. Maybe you're not even related."

"What was I doing when you shot me?" he demanded.

"I didn't see you."

"What do you mean you didn't see me?" He strode closer, those brown eyes wild—and set on me. "How do you not see somebody standing in the middle of a herd of deer?"

"I don't know," I told him honestly. "That's part of the mystery."

"The mystery," he said bitterly.

"I mean, the—"

"Fine," he said, turning on his heel. "I know what you mean."

I waited and waited for Nick to turn around. For him to say something. What must be going through his mind? When it seemed like eternity had passed, and he didn't seem any closer to turning around, I murmured, "What now?"

He turned and shrugged. "Don't know." He rubbed his face, looking at me through his fingers. Then he pulled the paper out from under his arm and stared at it. I couldn't see his face, but I figured he was looking at the picture.

"I dunno," he said—almost a groan. "You think it looks like me?"

I chewed my lip. I did, but I wasn't sure whether to say so. "It looks a lot like you," I measured. "But people sometimes look alike. When you look at it, does it feel like you?"

"Not at all. I... don't think I have a family." He pulled his shoulders up and put a hand over his eyes. "It's not me. I just know it isn't."

"Okay." At the time, I would have said I didn't know why I told him, "You can stay with me until you figure it out... I mean, if you want."

He arched a brow. "I can't hide at your house forever."

"Actually," I said slowly, "I was thinking of going to a party tonight..."

"Go to your party."

"*And*, I was thinking you should come, too."

Those dark eyes narrowed. "That... You don't have to do that."

"I know I don't have to, but what if I want to?" It seemed absurd, considering the circumstances, but maybe it wouldn't be a bad thing. "I could tell people you're my cousin."

"Cousin Nick."

"Yeah."

His face had lightened a little, but it went stormy again.

"What?"

He shrugged. Nick-Gabe had the I'm-a-teenage-guy-and-I-don't-care shrug down. "What if people recognize me?"

"It's a costume party. Which means," I said, holding out my hand, "we get to go and buy disguises."

He stared at it—my hand—for several seconds before taking it. I tugged him toward the bike, and he waved me on first. He slid on behind me, gently encircling my waist. This time, his arms felt heavy.

Ella James

CHAPTER TWELVE

I drove to the costume shop. I wasn't as smooth as Nick was with the bike, but I trusted my driving more than his at the moment. A few minutes after I'd pulled back onto the road, I'd felt him lean more weight against me, his chest melding warmly to my back. As I drove, I wondered what was going through his mind. My own was a whirlwind of denials and sureties. Nick *had* to be Gabriel DeWitt. He looked exactly like the guy. I'd kept it light when he asked, but the truth was, if Nick wasn't Gabe, he was a clone.

The trouble was, him *being* Gabe DeWitt raised more questions than it answered. If they were going on a camping trip, why had he been wearing a tux? A starched, stain-free tux? And if their car rolled off a freakin' cliff during a freak landslide…Why didn't he have one single bruise? Not even so much as a hair out of place.

By the time I parked in front of Howland's Costume Booth—which had, over the years, grown big enough to fill a vacated supermarket building—I'd decided Nick had to be Gabe. I didn't know how he had survived or wandered onto my property unsoiled, but I knew Nick's—*Gabe's*—face when I saw it, and that had been him staring at me from the newspaper page.

Nick swung off the bike before I did. I reached for his arm, balancing my weight as I slid off. Instead of letting go when I got my footing, I laced my arm through his and threw my whole self into an effort to make our time together as pleasant as possible.

"This," I started, nodding at the building's long, dark purple awning, "is Howland's. We used to come here every year when I was little. I was a bunny, then a Ghost Buster, one year a Powerpuff girl. Blossom. Do you know who I'm talking about?"

"I do," Nick-Gabe—well, he was Nick for now—said.

"None of the Powerpuff Girls had brown hair, and I originally thought Blossom looked the most like me. Now that I re-think it, though, I figure I was Blossom cause she acts the most like me."

Nick held the door for me, and we walked into a fantasy paradise. The walls were striped with rows of flashing lights. The air smelled like bubblegum and plastic. I scanned the aisles, an idea for our costumes already forming; Nick pulled me through the security sensors and into a space between two racks.

"Look," he said earnestly. He was standing very close— close enough I could have pressed myself against him with just a tiny step forward. "I want you to know something."

"Okay…"

"I'm not him. Gabe." Nick pulled his arm free of mine, wiping his palms on the thick khaki hiking pants. "I wanted you to know, you don't have to feel sorry for me. I'm not Gabe DeWitt."

I nodded slowly. "Okay." I forced myself to shrug, to act like what he'd just said didn't scream *Denial!* in evil,

Disney-villain tones. "Okay," I said again. "That's good I guess."

I turned toward the store's long aisles. "Are you more like a banana or more like Donald Trump or Indiana Jones or... I don't know, something more abstract, like a supernova?"

Nick's eyes widened. Almost immediately he un-widened them.

"What'll it be?" I prodded, hoping he would talk to me—and not just about costumes. I was trying to be a good sport, but the truth was, I was seriously worried about him.

"Well," he said, "I definitely don't want to be a banana. No celebrities, either. Indiana Jones is all right, but I'm thinking we should look around."

"A guy who likes to shop." I smiled. "I bet you have a girlfriend."

The stupid part of me that still wanted to be Bella (the very small, kept secret from everyone part) suffered a stomach drop, but I was for the most part a reasonable girl. I knew I couldn't keep him forever. Even if I punched the voice that told me that in the throat.

We browsed the inanimate object area and passed into children's movies, where Nick cracked a tiny smile and tried to talk me into going as an Oompa Loompa ("I'll be Willy Wonka"). We moved through the scary creatures section, where he rejected my suggestion that he go as a vampire and I scoffed at his recommendation that I go as a witch-disguised-as-sexy-maid.

On aisle six, beside an elaborate arrangement of various sorts of Silly String, I found a bin of jelly eyeballs and threw one at him.

It hit him square in the shoulder. For a long second, Nick didn't move. *Oh, geez*, I thought. *He's realized he* is *Gabe.* When he strode past me, I knew he had. But when he turned around a second later, he was holding a Yoda suit.

He pressed it to me, and I couldn't help but laugh. "Yoda I am not! Really, you crazy boy. If anyone's going as someone old and wrinkly, it's you!"

Nick grabbed a light saber. I grabbed another. Fifteen minutes later, we were out of there with Leia and Luke costumes, and I was feeling inappropriately lighthearted considering the circumstances.

When we got back to the bike, I realized there was nowhere to put our costumes. Which led to Nick saying, "Let's put them on here."

Here turned out to be an ice cream parlor named Jimmy's Yummy, where Nick changed in the men's room and I ordered us two chocolate sundaes.

He emerged wearing Luke's signature white toga-like top over form-fitting tan pants, paired with my dad's old boots. A wide brown belt defined his waist. It seemed narrow compared to his wide shoulders. He pulled a light saber from the belt and whipped it through the air.

"Not too fast," I warned, standing with my own costume in hand. "You haven't escaped the moisture farm just yet."

"Oh, yeah? Who's gonna keep me there?"

"Maybe I should." I eyed his costume.

"Huh?"

"Never mind," I murmured. "Eat your ice cream. I didn't know what you liked, but you can get rid of the cherry," I called as I walked toward the girls' room. Good thing I was walking, too, because—again—my terrible word choice had turned my cheeks red.

The Leia costume was a form-fitting, long-sleeved, turtle-necked white dress, tall white boots, and a blaster. I'd added a light saber, which she didn't use in the films, but the store didn't have a Generic Female Jedi costume.

I worked my hair into loose braids, then used a pack of bobby pins to mold them into circles on each side of my head. When I examined the mirror and saw how tight my dress fit, I again felt a lot like not myself.

I couldn't help but think that was because of Nick.

When I walked out, he was smiling blissfully into his ice cream bowl.

"Amazing," he said, with a lazy glance my way.

"Yeah, their sundaes are the best."

"I didn't mean their ice cream." He wiggled his eyebrows.

"Brother! How inappropriate!" I tried to smile, but it was hard when my brain was turning to mush.

"Ice cream's not bad, either," he added.

He pushed mine at me, and I ate it, glad for the cold to cool my cheeks.

Ella James

Chapter Thirteen

Annabelle Monroe lived in a castle. No, really. Her house was a replica of a sixteenth century Slovenian castle, copied stone-by-stone by her retired Hollywood costume-designer dad.

Mr. Monroe was pretty ancient—80, people joked, but actually 62—and since Annabelle's mom had left them both when we were in sixth grade, the old guy traveled all the time.

Annabelle had a housekeeper, Lora, who was supposed to double as a nanny, but Lora had a problem with narcolepsy, and Annabelle had no qualms about slipping Lora a sleeping pill and bidding her goodnight in her teenie tiny room, a tower modeled after the original castle's servant quarters.

Annabelle's bedroom was the largest tower, and I'd heard it was elaborate. I'd seen Lora's room once when Halah had dragged me to Annabelle's to pick up some cheer shoes, but I wasn't tight enough with Annabelle to see "The Lair."

As I steered down the winding, tree-lined driveway, my mind was on the stiff figure behind me. I wondered for the hundredth time since we'd left Jimmy's Yummies whether this was a mistake. Would Nick have fun? *Could* he have fun, with things the way they were? Beyond that, *should* he—when his whole family was probably dead? He was in denial, but I wasn't.

And what had happened to *me*? I wasn't a goody two-shoes or anything, but I was typically responsible. If you ignored the whole continue-my-dad's-research-in-secret business, which, I remembered, was kind of how everything started in the first place.

So maybe this wasn't completely about Nick.

Spotlights made the castle glow like a brilliant, rocky planet. It winked through the fanned limbs of enormous fir trees. Valets shone flashlights at arriving cars, directing them into two lots: one beside the house (actually the remnants of a private airport) and another beside the Monroes' tennis courts.

From the look of the airport lot, half the school was already there. I saw a long-tailed dinosaur, a princess with a glowing wand, a stem of balloon-grapes, and several pirates as a valet waved Nick and me down a pale stone path that seemed to disappear into the mountainside.

"Park by the other bikes," he yelled.

I turned between two maple trees, happy to park somewhere secluded. Our final destination was a tiny courtyard, complete with a topless mermaid fountain; two other bikes stood under a tall cliff side: a battered Harley and a souped-up Kawasaki—of the kind Dad used to call crotch rockets.

I cut the power on the Agusta and turned around. "You ready?" I asked softly.

Nick raised his light saber.

I took my helmet off, and the soft bass thump grew louder. The air was cold and almost damp; it seemed to hang like a sheer curtain around us.

I'd never taken Nick for shy, but as we walked I was surprised he didn't seem more nervous. Maybe he was finally thinking about other things. I quashed another burst of worry—worry that he'd face the truth at the party and somehow embarrass himself. I'd stick close by, just to make sure.

I grabbed his hand after we stepped onto the manicured front lawn, tugging him back into the bushes. "Just a sec," I said. I fished my cell phone out of my Leia suit's pocket and sent my mom a text. She knew about the party, but she probably had forgotten. Then I checked my missed call log: twenty-seven. Geez.

I scrolled through my unread texts: two from S.K., nine from Halah, one from Bree, and one from Mom ("b hm 18 tonite"). Then I flipped my phone shut.

"Okay."

I took Nick's arm the way I had outside of Howland's— this time to soothe myself, not him. I liked big parties maybe once or twice a year, but mostly I went for my friends.

"You're my cousin, remember," I said as we followed a pebble trail around the castle.

"Cousin Nick from East Egg?"

"Let's have you be from... Where's somewhere you know a lot about?"

Nick shrugged. "Pick a place."

"St. Louis."

"I can do that."

"Really?"

Nick nodded.

I squeezed his arm as we approached two large, mahogany double doors. "Remember if you want to leave, just let me know. And don't disappear, okay?"

"Jedi promise," he said.

"Is there one?"

"No. But I think they'd probably frown on lying."

The doors opened to a massive foyer two floors high with a huge, turquoise chandelier hanging from the roof. There was a formal dining room to the left—with an extra long, extra fancy claw-footed table and some porcelain sculptures that looked more expensive than some people's homes—but it was closed off by a Japanese partition wall.

We passed through the massive living space—the great room's walls also rose two floors above us; its ceiling was deep blue and glittered like there were tiny diamonds on it. There were so many rooms, I didn't know the names for all of them. They were decorated like you'd imagine: paintings I'd seen before, in lavish frames, the heads of animals Mr. Monroe had killed, more sculptures... One room—a giant martini bar—was devoted to Andy Warhol. A sitting room was done in Scottish Highlands décor, complete with a cabinet full of scotch. Finally we passed through a long hall lined with plants and reached a wall of windows that, on second glance, were doors to the deck.

The deck was two levels; we were on the first, where the bass was loud enough to make your head explode. This was the dance floor, obviously. Probably half the party was there, bumping together, making it impossible to squeeze through without holding Nick's hand. The deejay's booth was on our right, and there were fog machines and dozens of lights; they squiggled colors and shapes across the air, against the mountain face, then rained down a rainbow of starlight over the crowd.

We walked up some stairs behind a wall with a movie projection and were immediately assailed by a dance train. Nick jerked me out of the way just in time to avoid getting trampled.

I smiled my thanks. He smiled back, almost managing to look lighthearted.

I took out my cell to text S.K.—I would never find my gang in this place without a little help—but before I could open it, something hard bumped into my side.

"Miloooooooo!"

I jerked around, surprised to see Annabelle. Wait a second—was that Annabelle? She looked like a freakin' model. She had on a white dress like mine, but rather than a dorky turtle neck and long sleeves, hers was sleeveless and super short; the barely there skirt hung in jagged pieces over her muscular, tanned thighs. A thick, gold belt encircled her waist, round gold earrings hung from her ears, and she wore a snake-shaped golden band around her thin bicep. But what really made the outfit was her hair. It shone like molten gold, piled on top of her head in a series of elaborate knots; some pieces hung down around her neck for an effect that almost reminded me of snakes.

"Milo!" she cried, bumping me with her hip. She jumped away and sprung into a jumping-jack pose that made her small, lithe body look more elegant than mine would in a pirouette. "Who am I, Milo? Can you guess?"

She sprung back toward me and pulled her hair off her

neck, exposing twin red marks. I frowned, confused. A vampire-bitten figure skater, sans skates?

"Cleopatra!" she squealed.

I knew the exact moment she noticed Nick beside me. All the excitement faded off her face, and Annabelle's pretty hazel eyes narrowed suspiciously. Her tone changed, too. From honey sweet to deep and sharp. "Milo, honey, who is this?"

I turned toward Nick, feeling possessive.

"This is my—" friend, I was going to tell her.

But Nick beat me to the punch. Pulling his arm out of mine, he stretched it out for Annabelle to grasp. "I'm Milo's cousin, Nick, from St. Louis."

Annabelle squealed again. She didn't just grab Nick's hand. She threw her body at it. The result was that Nick accidentally groped her perky boobs. Annabelle didn't seem to notice—or care.

"Cousin *Nick*!" she squawked, threading one of those thin hands through his hair. "Nice to meeettt you!" She tousled his hair more, actually bumping me out of the way as she did. "Your hair is just like mine!" she cried. "It's beautiful!" She laughed, her signature throaty sound. "We're goddesses! Wait... You're a god. A ginger god! I'm a golden goddess!" She stumbled back, checking Nick out like she wanted to eat him. "Are you Han Solo?"

"Luke Skywalker," Nick said with a tiny smirk.

She giggled, and I belatedly realized Annabelle was drunk off her ass.

"You're Luke, and I'll be Padmé!"

Eww. Luke's *mother*?

Nick just chuckled.

I avoided scowling by the narrowest of margins and grabbed Nick's hand. "Annabelle, I want to introduce Nick to Halah. Have you seen her?"

Annabelle nodded happily, and pointed to the stone ceiling above us. "Top deck. Doing Jello shots and *things*." She grinned—at Nick, not me. "What a bad, bad girrrl."

I'd expected to have to wrestle Nick away from her, but just then, Carlos Farr (as Neil Armstrong) walked by, and Annabelle launched herself at him.

I tugged Nick toward the stairwell. "Sorry," I said, taken by a sudden—generous—impulse to take up for poor Annabelle. "She's... on the rebound."

Nick just laughed.

The sound system was wired so the stairwell walls were peppered with big, round speakers. As a result, I couldn't actually talk to Nick until we emerged onto the next deck, a torch-lit barbecue area where staff handed out neon glow necklaces and people danced in clusters.

Nick, I noticed, had grabbed hold of my sleeve sometime on the walk up the stairs—probably when we'd passed a group of rowdy, jersey-clad sophomore guys. He was standing close to me, and I felt a happy little rush.

"You doing okay?" he asked, and I laughed.

"Aren't I supposed to ask you that question?"

He smiled, and to my shock, he laced his hand through mine, bouncing my fingers with the tips of his. "I'm fine here," he said. "You're the one who's uncomfortable."

"I am? And how do you know that?" I squeezed his hand; my heart was pounding.

"I don't know," he said, his fingers teasing mine. "You're different here."

"Bad different?"

"No," he said. "Like…shy."

I yanked my hand from his and lightly punched his shoulder. "I'm not shy." Just then, I wasn't. I'd been possessed by someone older, surer, happier. I wasn't sure I recognized this Milo, and that was fine with me.

Anyway, what did it matter how I was with Nick? It would all be over soon. He'd go back to his life, and I'd stay here in mine.

"I'm glad you came here with me, cuz."

Nick's eyes held mine, and for a second, my heart stopped beating. "I'm not your cuz."

"Who are you?"

"I'm your friend—or something. Yeah?"

Or something. "Yeah. Of course."

We moved across the deck toward the smell of roasted pork, walking so closely our arms brushed with every step.

Before we reached the big pit fire, I heard my name and turned to find myself face-to-face with a lanky, dark-haired Ninja.

"S.K.!"

She grinned. "Leia."

S.K. snaked her hand around my neck, then noticed my escort. She pulled away from me, her angular face drawn in a frown. "Luke Skywalker," she said deeply, striking a ninja pose. "Confess your true identity or face the wrath of my dark arts."

I pulled my hand from Nick's, and had my mouth open to blurt something out when Nick said, "I'm her cousin."

"Cousin…" She shook her head. "Cousin you are not."

"Friend you are?" Nick asked.

S.K. giggled at his Yoda voice—it really was right on— and then said, "I'm her friend, but who are you?"

"My cousin," I said, smiling.

She knew I was lying, of course, but we never got a chance to hash it out. In that way that people have of popping up at parties, Halah and Bree appeared the next second. Bree, a blueberry muffin, lightly slapped my Leia hair, while sexy witch Halah grabbed S.K.'s arm and got all pink and giggly at the sight of Nick.

"Who are you?" she asked mysteriously.

S.K.'s brows arched. "This is Nick," she said, "Milo's cousin."

"Milo's cousin Nick…"

"I don't know of a cousin named Nick," Bree said.

And Halah leaned forward, grabbing Nick's chin. "Actually," she murmured, "I think I've heard of cousin Nick before."

The first sparks of jealousy were firing in my chest, but I'd had no time to reconcile our story before Annabelle appeared again—this time surrounded by a mob of giddy cheerleaders. Below us, someone cranked the music even louder, and I was only able to make out something about "Bobby's balls" before Annabelle lunged toward me, stealing Nick's light saber, then his hand.

"Anakin," she yelled, her fake eyelashes flitting like big bugs. "Do you want to see my lair?!"

Surprising myself, I grabbed Nick's other hand, but Annabelle yanked so hard she won the tug-o-war.

Without a backward glance, Nick let himself be stolen.

The two of them were engulfed in a sea of cheerleaders, moving toward the other end of the deck—the spot where it attached to the castle. At the top of the castle, I saw six towers—the largest one closest to us; its pink curtains glowed red.

The little hooker, I thought, fuming. I started stomping after them, but Halah grabbed my arm and handed me a beer.

"Leia, my dear. Why don't you try this dazzling refreshment? I think you need something to cool your temper. And your lady parts," she hissed, and then let out a giggle.

"You're drunk."

"Ding, ding, ding! Annnnd she's done it again, ladies and gentlemen!" Halah slapped my back, and S.K. stepped between us.

The music was so loud, she had to speak right into my ear. "Who is that guy? He's not your cousin."

I nodded; what else could I do? Halah opened my beer and shoved it at me, and I took it, if just to keep her from spilling it all over me. Her pointy hat bobbed as she started dancing, and a millisecond later, The Cheater Bobby came along and yanked her to his shoulder.

S.K. and I watched, open-mouthed, as Halah pushed her hips into his.

"I think she took something." That was Bree.

S.K. nodded. She squeezed my hand and spoke into my ear. "They're rolling!"

Great.

Annabelle had stolen my—my Nick, and she was probably drugging him with E.

I handed S.K. my beer, and she took it, looking concerned. "Hang onto this for me. I'll be back."

Chapter Fourteen

I squeezed through the crowd, parting the sea of bodies with my blaster, waving distractedly at people I knew who were sober enough to know that they knew me. Annabelle's parties had been intense before, but usually not like this. By the roasting hog, I saw men in white uniforms hauling empty kegs away. I wondered how much Mr. Monroe had to pay them to serve alcohol to high schoolers.

As I moved, I was conscious of my pounding heart, my sweating palms. I had a vision of Nick with Annabelle, lying on a pile of cushions while she lifted her trashy Cleopatra skirt. Then I saw Nick! Right in front of me.

He was dancing with April Dutton, a pretty senior gymnast with short black hair and brown eyes as hypnotic as Nick's. The sight of them together made my chest squeeze. Then Nick saw me—and pulled away.

He came over to me and grabbed my hand, looser than I'd seen him yet. "Milo. Hey." He smiled a little ruefully. "You've got some persuasive friends."

"Yeah," I said. "Guess so."

For some reason, I didn't feel grateful for his boomerang. Now that I had him back, I just felt annoyed.

I looked up at him, so smooth and sure of himself. So

hot. Then I pulled my hand from his and turned toward S.K. and Bree. "Have fun," I said over my shoulder. He could dance with whoever he wanted.

Before I could get two steps, Nick grabbed my wrist. "Wait. Where're you going?"

I shrugged, trying and failing to be casual, and before I could think of a way to spin my behavior as anything other than petty, Nick put his arms around me and pulled me close.

I hadn't noticed until then, but the music had gone slow and kind of quiet—some R&B song I didn't know. I smelled alcohol on Nick, and the moment of coziness was ruined.

"Did you have a drink?" I asked him, unnerved by the weight of his arms around my waist.

"Annabelle," he said. I hated the way he said her name, so melodic. So pretty.

"She spilled on you?"

His eyebrow arched. "Rebound, right?"

"Something like that."

I waited a second, feeling his hands on my back, weighing the pros and cons of what I was about to say. Then I said it. "I think you might know this, but if Annabelle gives you anything… Like, a pill."

Nick pulled a tiny shamrock from his pocket. "3, 4 Methylenedioxymethamphetamine, an entactogenic drug known colloquially as E. Enhances serotonin and…" He made a circle with his hand.

I narrowed my eyes. "I was going to say you shouldn't take it, but it's up to you I guess."

He smirked. "I think that's the last thing we need."

We swayed to the music, and Nick started stroking my hip. My skin was burning; then I imagined him with

Annabelle and felt a wave of misery. Then another rush of heat as he pulled me even closer.

"What's wrong?" he murmured.

"Nothing."

"You sure?"

What could I say? I'd gone insane. I forced a smile. "I just don't like these things—like you said."

"Then we should leave."

"No. It's no big deal."

I looked down, because I could feel that dark gaze on my face. Like I could feel his chest an inch from mine. My hands, around his neck, felt cool; his neck was hot and firm and smooth. I glanced up at his face and felt like I was on a roller coaster.

While I took deep breaths and tried to determine when exactly I'd gotten such a stupid crush, Nick pulled me fractionally closer. His eyes, when I got the nerve to glance at them, were closing. He ran his hand up my bare neck and I forgot to breathe.

We stood that way—entwined—until the song ended.

My head was buzzing with that same feeling, the same sense that Milo...that I knew her. That she was part of something. Staring at her face, I felt a hazy sense of purpose, one somehow at odds with myself, but at least I felt it.

I felt other things, too; the kinds of things a 17-year-old would normally feel when a beautiful girl was pressed against him. I practically jumped backward, and Milo stumbled a step forward. She was surprised, breathing hard, and I fumbled for something to say.

"I…"

Was interrupted by Milo's friend—the one in the karate uniform; S. K. She tugged Milo's sleeve and leaned in to whisper in her ear.

I couldn't make out what was said. It must have been unpleasant, because the dark-haired girl's eyes were wide, and her mouth was pulled into a worried frown.

Milo nodded, then turned to me. "I've got something I need to do." She hesitated. "It would probably be best if you waited here." I could tell she didn't like the idea. I wanted to reassure her, but all I could manage was "Okay."

"I'll be back in a sec, and then we can leave."

I felt bad, that she was leaving because of me, but more than that I felt too close to understanding, my desire to know choked by my fear.

I lifted my hands from my sides, wanting to shove them into the pockets of my tux, but of course, they didn't have much use for pockets on Tatooine. I stepped back into the shadow of the ivy-covered wall and watched as Milo and her friend neared the other side of the deck, where the third amigo—the curly haired girl, Halah—was slumped into an iron chair.

A second later, something else caught my eye: our hostess, Annabelle; she was crossing the deck, in long, furious strides, headed straight toward me.

The dance floor parted for her, like she was magic. Something dramatic must have happened, because when she was ten feet from me (*114.7 inches*), her face crumpled and she started to cry.

Then she staggered, and looked like she might face plant

right beside me; I stepped into her path and held out my hand. I expected her to veer the other way, but instead she threw herself at me and buried her face in my chest.

She said something I couldn't understand, then started pulling me inside.

"What?"

"I said, 'Do you wanna come and see my bedroom, Anakin?'"

CHAPTER FIFTEEN

As far as parties went, this one had to be the worst. First Annabelle had thrown herself at Nick. Then Halah and Annabelle had decided to roll, and in a fit of drug-fueled lust, Halah had locked onto The Cheater Bobby. Naturally, Bobby was thrilled to get attention from the girl who'd led the charge against him in paintball. The creep probably knew she was high; he didn't care. Inevitably, Annabelle had seen the two of them together, and she'd slapped Halah in the face.

Halah had cried, and then decided she was leaving, which was when S.K. had gotten me. We couldn't let her drive; she'd probably wrap her car around a phone pole. Then, apparently, when I left Nick, Annabelle had swooped in and stolen him. Now I was climbing the stairs to "The Lair."

There were elevators, of course, but someone had fired up a water bong on the fourth floor, and now all the elevators were jammed with bong traffic.

As I hiked the narrow stone stairs, my fury simmered. Nick thought he could dance with me *like that* and then run off with Annabelle?

Even better question: What did I care? He wasn't my boyfriend. I didn't know who the heck he was. Maybe he danced with everyone *like that*. Maybe wherever he was from, he had a bunch of girlfriends. Maybe he was so well liked that no one cared. The girls felt grateful when he deigned to look their way. Maybe I'd been thinking about Nick the wrong way all this time.

By the time I reached the fifth floor, my leg muscles were trembling and my Leia boots were permanently creased at the ankles.

As I searched for a door that looked like Annabelle's, I told myself that it didn't matter what I found behind it. Nick was no one to me. Nothing but a…what? A really weird coincidence. A trespasser, in fact!

I probably wouldn't have found Annabelle's room among the many huge, wooden doors on the fifth floor, but the hallway outside it smelled like perfume—the heavy, sickly sweet kind that has always reminded me of candied mosquito repellant.

I knocked, softly at first, then so hard my knuckles ached. When I didn't hear a sound, I felt a little sick. That could only mean one thing, right? The quiet? Then again, maybe that kind of thing was loud. Stupid me. I didn't even know.

I knocked again; just one more time, I told myself. Only this time, I knocked so hard, the door swung open.

It was dark, and I was at the bottom of a winding staircase. It was fourteen steps up and around, and this time the door I found was partially open. The room behind it was dimly lit and pink. Hot pink.

I held my breath, but I didn't hear anything—especially not *those* kinds of sounds. I knocked, but didn't wait for an answer. I pushed the door open, but stopped at the threshold, shocked.

Holy crap. What the heck happened here?

Annabelle's room was round, pink, and a disaster. Like a hippo had ransacked a department store and thrown up bubblegum all over the walls.

My eyes traveled over her delicate, off-white, antique furniture: makeup table, wash stand, entertainment system...bed.

Everything, everywhere had been pulled from its rightful place and jumbled on the floor, a colorful storm of clothes, jewelry, perfume bottles, DVDs, school books, shoes, underwear, soda cans, wadded up pieces of tissue, everything. There were even things hanging from the overhead fan, and a large, white antique dresser had been split in two.

Annabelle's garbage can, make-up chair, and coat rack were overturned. A canvas painting lay atop the garbage can, one of its corners punched in.

"Hello?" I called.

When no one answered, I looked once more at the bed, covered with a sheer, pink canopy. Then I stepped through the cracked door to my right: the bathroom.

I saw the puddle before I saw Nick. It was still bubbling, a shimmering pool of gold nail polish that was boiling across half the stone floor.

The rest of the bathroom was wrecked, and in the middle of the rubble, Nick knelt with his head in both his hands.

"Nick?"

He moaned, curling over into himself.

I picked my way through the mess with my heart in my knees. When I reached his side, he latched onto me and kind of fell, dropping his forehead onto my shoulder.

"Milo..."

His body trembled. I wrapped my arms around his shoulders, holding him tight. "Nick, are you okay?" I spoke into his ear, while one of my hands roamed up and down his back. "C'mon," I urged. "Tell me what happened."

He made another moan-ish sound—I felt his warm breath through my shirt—and my mind spun. What the hell could have happened in the five minutes—tops!—that they were up here? And how?

I glanced down at Nick, overwhelmed by rage at Annabelle, jealousy over the same, guilt for not preventing this, concern for Nick, anger at him, and—

Finally, Nick lifted his head, but instead of looking at me—instead of explaining—he crawled over to the toilet and got sick. I turned away to give him privacy, and my eyes landed on the puddle. It had finally cooled enough that I could tell what it was.

Not gold-colored nail polish. *Actual gold.*

I was stunned. The puddle on the floor—Halah had told me once about this solid gold angel Annabelle had in her bathroom.

"Ridiculous," Halah had called it.

I mumbled the word as I stared at it. I couldn't comprehend.

I turned when I heard Nick stumble to the sink, and waited by him while he washed his face. His eyes, when he looked at me, were red.

"Milo. I'm sorry," he rasped.

He looked beyond me at the puddle and took a big step back, bumping into the counter. He clutched the side of it with one hand, the other one going to his mouth.

"Oh, God."

He turned back to the counter, putting both of his hands on it and leaning on his arms with his head dropped in between them.

"God." I thought he would keep saying that forever.

"I think we need to leave," I said.

Nick turned. "I've got to—"

"No, you don't!" I grabbed his arm. "What you need to do is come with me. Where is Annabelle?"

Nick's face bleached white. "I... I left her on the bed."

I went cold all over. I jerked him into Annabelle's room and leaned him against a wall. I was trembling as I walked to the bed, but Nick brushed past me. He yanked the curtains open and leaned over the prone form behind them.

Annabelle was limp and gray, and to my eyes she looked dead. I checked her pulse. No pulse. *No pulse.*

"Shit!" I said, pressing my fingers into her neck. My heart was beating so hard I thought it might explode.

"Oh, shit, Nick, we've got to go."

He stayed by her bed, actually reached down and touched her face.

"What the hell are you doing?! Come on. We've got to *go, right now*!" I grabbed him by the wrist. He moaned, like being tugged behind me hurt, but I didn't slow. I couldn't. We needed to get out of there. I couldn't think. I couldn't breathe. We took the stairs down, both stumbling, and curse words kept pouring from my lips. Nick's life was... over. And Annabelle? My mind refused to go there.

By the time we reached the bike, Nick was trembling again and slumped on me. I closed my eyes and prayed for

Annabelle. Then we sped off—criminals, or worse.

Chapter Sixteen

I stopped at a dark park and text'd Sara Kate with shaking fingers.

Nick n I left. Take care of Halah, K?

Then I turned around to look at Nick. His arms were still around my waist. His eyes were wide, his auburn hair a mess.

"What happened?" I asked, my voice wobbly. "You've gotta tell me everything."

People had seen Nick go upstairs with her. He was the last one to see her...okay. I couldn't bring myself to think *alive*.

Nick swallowed, his face contorting. "I don't know," he said; his voice cracked.

"You have to know."

He looked down at his arms. "She wanted me to go upstairs. She was crying and she seemed really out of it." He inhaled. Exhaled. "I put her on her bed. I went into the other room—the bathroom—Shit." Nick pulled his arms away from me and grabbed his head. When he looked back up, his eyes were huge. "Did you see the floor?" The words trembled out. "It was like...this golden statue."

I nodded, then managed a raspy, "Yeah." I wished I was good at cursing, because yeah wasn't even close to the right word.

"When I saw it—It was just like at the rock. I got a bad headache. I went somewhere else. I started seeing numbers. And then the statue melted, and you were there, and stuff was everywhere. And Annabelle was—"

He didn't say it, so I had to. "I think she might be dead."

"No," Nick whispered. "She's not dead."

"How do you know?"

"I just do."

I remembered when he touched her face. I couldn't believe I was about to ask this. "You…did something?"

"Yeah," he mumbled. "I did something…" Again, he swept his hands back through his hair.

I felt relieved and shocked, at once. "Well what did you do?"

"I don't know. I'm sorry. I don't know. I don't know how. I touched her, and I could see her start to breathe again. I think I touched that statue, too."

"Touched her? What does that—"

"I don't know!" He was off the bike, pacing with his hands balled into fists. "I don't know what happened. I just don't."

A part of me wanted to go to him, but another part—a leery, self-preserving part—kept me on the bike.

Nick shook his head, his face grown grave. "Maybe I should go."

"Go where? That's not the problem. Things aren't going to get better with location. You need to tell me what is going on. *You* are the only one who knows. If you don't tell me…I can't help you."

He shook his head, like I just didn't get it. Maybe I

didn't.

"Did you take something?" I asked suddenly; I actually hoped he had.

He laughed, the sound like crunching leaves. "I wish."

But you didn't. And that meant I was in way over my head.

I thought about leaving. For just a second, I thought about getting on the bike and taking off. Annabelle had died—I had seen her *dead*—and I wasn't sure I would ever stop seeing her.

Nick stood with his jaw locked, looking at his boots, pressing the tip of one into the curbside.

"How did you melt the statue?" I asked him quietly. "How did you bring someone back to life? And why did she—" I still couldn't say it. "What happened to her?"

He turned to face me. "What do you think?"

I didn't answer because I didn't want to think about it.

"Do you remember...getting to her room?"

"I remember her tripping, going up the stairs. I was worried."

"So you...what? Ransacked her room and decided to melt a statue? How did these things happen? You don't have *any* idea?"

He shut his eyes. "Something is wrong with me."

"I'd say."

His face flickered with something that looked a lot like hurt, but he quickly snuffed it out. "Thank you for the ride to town. I think it's clear you didn't do this with your dart."

He turned, like he was going to walk away, and anger flared like a match inside my chest. "*No.* You can't just leave."

When he faced me again, his face had changed. No longer hard, he just looked tired. "What should I do then, Milo?"

My throat tightened, and the words were out before I had time to think. "Come with me."

Nick folded his arms and shook his head. "I don't think that's a good idea."

My heart pounded. "Why?"

"I need to go somewhere...alone. Until I figure out whatever this is."

"And how are you going to do that? Find enlightenment in the forest?" He ignored me, and I sighed. "Maybe you're an angel, like that statue."

He eyed me warily. "I don't think so."

I sat up straighter. "There's got to be something we can do to get it figured out. Something we can read..."

"Yeah, we can Google it." Nick rolled his eyes, looking totally un-Nick-like. Looking miserable.

"Why don't you get back on the bike? I'm not leaving you here."

He looked over his shoulder, at the clump of urban forest behind him—and I *knew* that look. "Don't," I warned, climbing off the bike and walking slowly toward him.

When I got close enough, I grabbed his hand. He let me, but he didn't touch me back. He just stood there, and when I stroked his fingertips, his eyes slid shut.

A few seconds later, he stepped away. "Look...I'm never going to feel like Gabriel DeWitt. The only thing that makes me feel like a...real person is...you." He rubbed a hand through his coppery hair and swallowed, Adam's apple bobbing. "But I don't want you to get hurt."

"How could I get hurt?"

"I don't know. Why don't you ask your friend?" He rubbed his forehead, looking less gathered than I'd ever seen him.

I still had my hand out. I wanted to reach for him again, but I could tell he'd move away, so I just stood there, vibrating.

"It's the same for both of us. We're in the same boat, Nick. We don't know what's going on." I thought about the boy who'd lost his whole family and my throat went tight. "You said you thought you knew me. Maybe we can…" I didn't know what to say. We were at a dead end, but I knew I couldn't let him disappear.

He met my eyes with his hard, dark ones. "You don't have to help me anymore."

"I know."

CHAPTER SEVENTEEN

As soon as we got safely to my room, I called S.K., who said something that made my head feel like a hot-air balloon: Not only was Annabelle alive, but apparently she had reappeared to finish her catfight with Halah.

"She's not just *okay*," I told Nick, with a wild giggle. "She was so good, she went back down to fight with Halah!"

Nick just looked at me. He was sitting on my bed, leaning against the pillows, playing idly with a Rubik's Cube. His hand around it now was clenched, the knuckles white.

He looked so messed up, I couldn't stand it. But the truth was, I couldn't bring myself to really dig into things. What would I even say? I was clueless, and I definitely didn't want to make him more upset.

"I'm going to change, okay?"

He nodded.

"Why don't you lie down?"

I didn't wait to hear his answer, just grabbed some clothes from my closet and shut myself inside the bathroom, where I sat down on the tub's ledge and wondered what the H was going on.

There was something wrong with him. Something really

wrong. That much was obvious. Some part of me knew that I should kick him out—send him packing. Whatever was going on was strong enough to melt pure gold, and I didn't know if I could handle it.

But a larger part of me—the part of me coming out of a two-year crash—wanted to see what happened next. And really wanted to join him on the bed.

I took a deep breath. *Focus*. Legit weirdness was going down. Whatever had happened at the party, it had hurt him. Made him sick. It was something he didn't understand, something he hadn't asked for. Therefore it wasn't his fault. Right?

I returned to my room ready to talk things out. Ready to offer my support. Ready to get to the bottom of whatever was going on. Instead, I found Nick slouched against the pile of pillows, the Rubik's Cube resting on his knee, solved, his head lolled back, beauty in the lamplight.

I pulled his shoes off, covered him with a fleece blanket, and double-checked my door. Satisfied that it was locked, I settled in the rocking chair and opened my laptop. I went to Facebook, then searched for Gabe DeWitt. I looked at Nick's face, Gabe DeWitt's smiling profile pic. And that was all I could see. The profile, like Nick himself, was locked.

The next morning, I awoke in bed. Nick was on the floor, propped against the wall, looking like a punk-rock model in what remained of his tattered tux.

Before I could thank him for putting me in bed—before I could get over the fact that Nick had picked me up from the chair and put me in my bed—he looked hard into my eyes and said, "I think that I should go."

Call me crazy, but that struck me as a terrible idea.

"Go where?" I asked him dumbly.

"Where do you think?"

"To New Castle?"

He nodded. "Janice DeWitt's house."

"Your—I mean *Gabe's* grandmother. "

"Yes."

I held my breath for a long second, trying to stop myself from saying *no*! Nick couldn't leave. I didn't want him to. And that was 100 percent selfish.

"Did you remember…something about…Gabe DeWitt?"

Nick just stared at me, his jaw set tight.

"I'm sorry," I said gently. "Nick, I'm really sorry."

I slid out of bed, headed to him, but Nick was faster. He was at the deck door before I could get close.

"Nick—Gabe, hang on. Wait."

I'd have to go downstairs, tell my mom bye, and get the keys to the car. I wouldn't take him to New Castle on the bike. We needed to talk. Even if he had remembered he was Gabe, it didn't explain the whistle, the melted statue, the thing with Annabelle. It didn't explain how he was alive. I knew I had to let him go, but not without some kind of resolution.

"Will you wait here for me? Please? I want to talk before you go, but I've gotta tell my mom I'm leaving. After that I'll take you. I'll meet you around back, by the car."

Nick-Gabe nodded, his face a gorgeous mask.

I went downstairs and found Mom scrambling eggs. She seemed cheery. "Thank God for high-dollar mechanics!" She grinned, and I realized the turbines were back up—all our power was restored. It should have occurred to me, since I had been able to search the Web.

I looked over at the TV, a creepy-crawly feeling shuddering through me. "Mom, I have a question... Did you put the TV on the solar panel circuit?"

"No, honey. Why?"

I swallowed hard. "No reason." I made my face neutral, my tone casual. "Hey, may I take the car to town? I left my purse at Annabelle's."

It wasn't a lie. In the chaos of the night before, when Nick and I had—oh, God—fled what I had thought was some kind of crime scene, I'd forgotten my purse. I squeezed my eyes shut.

"Sure you can," Mom said. "Does that mean you don't have a phone?"

"I do," I told her, turning so she couldn't see the strain on my face. "Call me later."

Mom nodded, saying something I didn't hear as I slipped out the door. I walked around the house, my eyes searching for Nick. I found him in the car, passenger's side. He was playing with the seam at the bottom of his dress shirt. He didn't look up as I got settled, and he didn't speak as I sped down the driveway, taking a sharp turn onto Mitchell Road.

As I drove, away from my ridge of the Front Range, toward the shallower valleys of New Castle, I could feel the tension wafting off my passenger like summer heat off pavement.

By the time I made the turn onto Highway 6, toward I-70 and New Castle, I was wracking my brain for a conversation-starter.

"So, I'm some kind of freak," Nick said abruptly. After so much silence, his voice shocked me: like always, so deep and smooth and lovely.

"The kind that can do really awesome things."

"I destroyed her room," he said. "I melted that thing, the angel."

My heart beat faster. "Do you have any idea—*how*?"

He shook his head. "I could have killed her."

"But you *saved* her."

"But did I kill her first?"

Chills sprung up on my arms at the question, and the flat tone with which he delivered it. It took me a second to get my breath. "Did you?"

"I don't think, but then, I don't remember, do I?"

He was silent for a second—a second in which I thought I'd go insane. When he spoke, his voice was tight. "Milo, I need to ask you something. Don't tell anyone about this. Okay?"

"Of course I won't. But are you going to?"

He bit his lip. "I don't think so. Not now." He exhaled roughly. Rubbed his face. "I don't know. What would I say? That I melted a statue?"

"Good point." People would have him committed.

The road in front of us rolled on, expanding into interstate as it took us over craggy hills, through wind-swept valleys, toward the one place that I didn't want to go. I thought about the miles between us—more than 100 of them—and wanted to turn the car around. Then I felt stupid for wanting that. What I should want was for this mess to be over.

I glanced at Nick again. "Should I be calling you Gabe

now?"

To my surprise, he shook his head. His face was hard. "I don't remember anything. And I still don't think I'm Gabe."

I hit the brakes—almost causing a truck to rear-end us. "Then why am I taking you to New Castle?! Why not stay with—"

"Because," he interrupted. "It's the only thing that I can do. This is the only lead I have."

"But if you're not Gabe DeWitt, how is he a lead?"

Nick pulled a torn newspaper page out of his pants pocket and held it out. I saw a photo of Gabe Dewitt and two other boys at some kind of swim meet. Embarrassingly, the black and white image made me warm.

Nick pointed to something I couldn't see, then he lifted his dress shirt. I saw a birthmark on his ribcage, dark pink-red and shaped like a cloud. I realized it was pictured in the paper, too.

"Oh," I breathed.

"Yeah... *Oh.*"

Nick crumpled the paper, tossed it at his feet, and shifted his torso to stare out the window. His back, to me, looked clenched and tense.

"Are you sure you want to do this?" I asked, hesitant.

He turned his head, the motion quick and hard. "Do I have another option, Milo? Do you think that I can stay with you forever?"

"No," I said, half whimper.

"Well that's good. Because I can't."

I nodded numbly, watching the curving road as the lanes blurred, one wide path that led to nowhere.

Chapter Eighteen

I was an idiot. Whatever and whoever else I was, I was an idiot, too. I watched Milo tighten her grip on the wheel, straighten her back and pull her elbows in, her gaze trained to the road and her lips smashed together, and I wished one of my pseudo-powers was rewinding time.

If I could, I would go back. How far? The beginning— the beginning I remembered, anyway. When I opened my eyes and I saw Milo's face against the crisscrossing of branches above us. I'd start right then. Maybe I would freeze time.

I stared down at my lap, replaying the part where Milo had protested taking me to New Castle. She felt responsible, probably, but maybe there was something more?

I hadn't lied; I really knew I wasn't Gabriel DeWitt, despite the birthmark and everything else. But I hadn't been completely honest with her, either. I remembered more of what happened than I let on.

Though remembered wasn't the right word.

After I'd moved Milo to her bed, I'd done a little work on her computer. Long story short, I'd found out I was as good with a computer as I'd been with the car and the bike— and the alarm system. Not to mention the cameras at

Annabelle's place.

The technology, I got. I was working on a theory. The one non-variable—the thing I knew for sure—was that something had happened to Gabe. Something that enabled him—his body—to survive a plunge off a 40-foot cliff. Something that had, by coincidence or systematic necessity, enabled Gabe to know and do strange things. Something that had also taken his memory. And created me.

Was this thing a "miracle?"

I didn't think so.

Is it in my pocket?

The burning whistle had brought me out of my statue-melting experience just moments before Milo arrived. Searing a hole through my pants, burning my leg, like it had done hers.

Something weird had happened to Gabe, something that had made him me—made him Nick…

Why could I melt gold? Why did I know everything about everything but me? Why did I feel so stifled, so trapped?

Why did I feel there was no way to untangle myself? (From what?)

Who were the others I had felt in my strange, abstract vision of Milo? The "we" of the web?

Who was I?

The question kept haunting me, because I had an answer in my head—the same one I'd had since I'd first realized the question. When I thought about it, I felt it so strongly it almost had a voice:

You're no one.

I looked out the window. Nothing but a bunch of hills and valleys, craggy and covered by fir trees. We passed signs for White River, and later, Edwards. I knew I should say something—should say sorry—but I couldn't bring myself to say anything.

I didn't want to go to Janice DeWitt's house. I knew it was practical to leave, it was the best thing to do, but I kept thinking about the reasons I didn't want to leave, like Milo in her Leia outfit, the way the turtle neck had hugged her chest. And the way she looked asleep, with her dark hair spilled around her face, her long eyelashes black against the paleness of her face. I thought about what she'd told me about her dad.

I remembered how she'd felt under my hands, when I'd wrapped my arms around her on the motorcycle. When I'd stood so close to her, dancing.

I thought about the feeling I got when I imagined never seeing her again. The sensation that I needed to break away from...something. The sense that knowing Milo meant I might end up doing something that was horrible.

What?

By the time we reached our exit, I felt cold all over.

I told Milo, "Sorry."

She said, "It's okay. I know you've got to be stressed out."

We drove a few miles, while I decided that I hated New Castle—so small and dingy, everything looking insubstantial, like a gust of wind could blow it away and turn the land back to crumbing rock.

I wished that would happen.

Milo asked me to get the GPS out of the glove box, and I put Janice DeWitt's address in. The mechanical male voice guided us to the place where we would part. And when Milo pulled up at a small yellow house with a big bay window in the front and a front yard with no trees, she fished around and found a pen and paper.

"I'm giving you my number," she said, looking at me with her big green eyes. "I want you to call me if you need anything, okay?"

I thought the words: *Don't tell,* and Milo didn't hear them but I think she felt the point.

"I'll keep everything a secret. No worries."

I nodded and I hugged her hard. As I walked through the yard, I tried to keep the feeling of her heat.

It was Thursday afternoon before I heard anything more of Gabe DeWitt. I'd gotten through Tuesday—our first day back at school after the teacher holiday—and Wednesday by avoiding the TV, the radio, and Internet news sites.

When Bree, Halah, and even Annabelle tried to ask about my cousin, I blew them off. I was so determined not to think of Gabe that in the mornings I got the books for all my classes so I could avoid the lockers—and my friends' questions—all together. Halah didn't remember much about "Nick," so she didn't press; she just said, "I know he's not your cousin." Annabelle was a little more insistent. She offered me $50 for Nick's phone number, then accused me of being on "Halah's side" when I wouldn't give it to her.

S.K. was the only one who knew a portion of the truth: that Nick was someone I'd met randomly, and for now, I didn't want to talk about him. When she asked me in the bathroom after our mutual honors history class, my eyes were red and puffy; when I brushed her off, she didn't press.

I actually might have confided in her on Thursday afternoon, but she left orchestra practice with ComicCon Ami The Xylophone Player from Mullen High before I could track her down and spill my guts.

Thursday night, a few minutes before 7 o'clock, I text'd Mom—she wasn't coming home for another hour or two—then made myself oatmeal for dinner and turned the TV to Channel Nine Action News.

Within minutes, Gabe's face was in the corner of my screen, and my heart was sinking.

The newscaster, an over-made-up woman with long black hair and the annoying habit of enunciating the wrong words, said things like "miraculous" and "extraordinary." His friends and family, she said, were "overjoyed" to have him back. Then she interviewed two girls and two boys, the two boys wearing the black and royal blue of Coal Ridge High School. I watched their faces, not even hearing what they said.

"Gabe's grandmother, *Janice* DeWitt, says he is looking forward to getting back to school, where he plays wide-receiver for the Titans. For *now*, Gabe remains at a Denver-area rehabilitation center, where he will work with specialists to regain his memory and, ultimately, get over the *strange* ordeal that spared his life—but not his *family*."

And then it was over. I turned the TV off and stared, feeling cheated. That woman hadn't told me anything!

I climbed upstairs and combed through online news stories. Apparently Gabe had told people that he'd come to miles from the crash site, and had discovered who he was when he wandered into town and saw his picture on a newspaper. Who dropped him off? A "stranger."

I felt irrationally upset—at being described as a stranger. I felt worse when, in another story that had been published on Sunday, a girl named Halley Sturgis was quoted saying she was "holding out hope." The newspaper had called her Gabe's girlfriend.

CHAPTER NINETEEN

On Friday, those of us performing with the Denver Youth Orchestra the next afternoon got the school day off. I slept until ten o'clock, intentionally leaving myself only 45 minutes before our marathon rehearsal started. I was sitting in my bed, staring at the Rubik's Cube that Nick *(Gabe!)* had solved, when I heard the doorbell ring.

I thought it was Nick *(Gabe!!)*.

Of course I did...

So before I ran downstairs, I brushed my teeth and combed my hair and swapped my dingy navy sweatpants for a pretty, pale pink pair. Before I tugged the door open, I smoothed my charcoal *Beam Me Up* t-shirt.

It wasn't Nick *(Gabe!!!)*.

Instead, I found myself face-to-face with two of the most serious-looking men I had ever seen. They wore identical suits—sleek, black, and starched beyond perfection—and identical frowns.

Ohhhhhhh, Men in Black was the first thing that I thought, and almost said it.

Lucky for me, I didn't, because the taller, darker one—a handsome African-American man two feet taller than me and three times as wide—fixed me with a death stare.

"Mrs. Mitchell?" he said. His voice was like a dog's bark: sharp and clear and startling.

I nodded, though of course, I wasn't Mrs.

He pointed to his sidekick, a younger man—I thought of him more as a "guy"—with blond hair and the kind of lean physique that made me think of park our. "This is Agent Diego. I'm Agent Sid." He reached into his pocket and pulled out an ID badge. Diego just stood there, looking smug.

"We're from the Department of Defense," he said, like that might mean something.

I nodded, stupid. "My mom is Mrs. Mitchell," I blurted. "She's up at the turbines." I swallowed, regretting that I'd told them that. "Is something wrong?"

"Something *was*," said Sid.

I waited a beat for him to explain, and Diego, the blond, stepped forward. "You are aware that the area recently experienced a large power outage?" I wanted to say, 'You mean the one that just happened like two days ago?', but nodded instead. "We're trying to find out why. Shouldn't take us long, but we need access to your property."

"Uh..." I was confused. What did the Department of Defense have to do with a power outage? I was trying to work up the courage to ask, when I glanced at Sid. His gaze left a trace of heat. "Okay..."

Sid nodded, and Diego said, "Okay."

I ran my palm over my hair. "Well, let us know if we can help. My mom or me."

Diego nodded.

I started to shut the door, but at the last minute I stuck my head back out. "Do you think we had something to do with it? I mean, the turbines?"

Diego said, "No," at the exact moment Sid said, "We can't be sure."

They exchanged a look—one where I couldn't tell who was chastising whom—and then nodded, in absolute unison. Then they turned away.

Rehearsals happened at Boettcher Hall, a concert hall in the middle of the Denver Performing Arts Center, right in the heart of downtown.

Boettcher is unusual because it's round. Concert halls usually aren't. Sitting on the stage, I usually feel like a fish in a bowl, even if the seats are empty. I keep it together during performances, but practices always kick my butt. That Friday, I messed up my part on the piano not because of nerves, but because my mind was somewhere else.

I thought about Nick, of course.

I'd been thinking about him almost every second since I'd dropped him off. But that morning, as I'd watched two black Tahoes drive toward the turbines, I thought again about the moment I found Nick. It had followed a flash of light. The power had been out when we got to my house.

The more I thought about that, the more loony I felt. Like I was being paranoid. Except what really made me paranoid was to write the whole thing off, as if it didn't matter. I felt so certain that it did. That Nick did.

His face kept swimming through my head, so instead of messing up once or twice, I botched my part all four times we ran through our stuff. I was so bad that Dr. Fawn pulled me aside afterward to ask if I had hurt my hands.

"Is it the piano?" he asked when I shook my head. "They've switched them out—you noticed that. The Steinway you usually use was mangled by some drunken Frenchman." Dr. Fawn wrinkled his blade-straight nose.

"I think it may be the piano," I lied. (Honestly, I hadn't even noticed). "I promise I'll do a better job tomorrow."

The thing about Dr. Fawn was, for a perfectionist, he could be seriously flighty. Not to mention unobservant. Any conscious person who didn't have his head completely up in space would have noticed I was not myself that day.

I'd taken Dad's Agusta to rehearsal, wanting to feel the cold smack of the wind, to feel like I had as much control over my life as I did over the bike. Control had always been my thing, going back to after Dad died and I decided not to eat about 95 percent of the world's foods, and ended up in Dr. Sam's office getting "therapy."

Of course, driving a motorcycle didn't solve my problems. By the time I turned onto Mitchell Road, I was feeling anxious and unhappy.

I sped up at the mailbox, wanting to *fly* down our driveway—and I was, when I noticed the black SUV, parked in the same place it had been four hours earlier.

Even at the speed of light, I could make out Sid and Diego's bleary figures standing on the doorstep. For a moment, I felt sure that our front door was open, but the next instant it was shut.

If I was paranoid then, it was worse when I parked the bike, tucked my sweater around myself, and climbed the front porch stairs.

Instead of Sid, this time Diego nailed me. He stuck out

his tanned arm and caught my hand like we were buds or something. "Milo," he said. "You got a second?"

"Um, sure." I extricated my arm, feeling somehow both rude and violated.

"You remember Saturday morning?" Diego asked.

Oh, crap.

"What were you doing?" I blinked at Diego's raspy, young-ish voice.

"Um, Saturday?" I sounded like a liar. Already. "Saturday morning... I guess I went to my old tree house." When my face got hot from lying, I shrugged and tried to exaggerate it. "Kind of dorky, I know. I go there sometimes, to relax."

"So you were outside when it happened?"

"...*It*?"

"The outage."

I shrugged. "I guess so."

Sid cut in. "Did you see anything unusual?"

I shook my head, frowning. (That much was not hard to do). "Like what?"

"Anything," Sid said firmly. "Anything at all."

I told them I'd seen some deer, but other than that, it had been an uneventful morning. A few minutes later, I shut the door behind me. In addition to shooting someone with a deer tranquilizer and leaving an acquaintance for dead, now I had lied to the Department of Defense.

Good stuff.

By eight o'clock, my mind was so boggled I could hardly see straight. I'd been wandering the house, Nick's Rubik's Cube in my hand, staring at walls and pictures. I should have been practicing on my keyboard. I could have turned on the TV news.

Instead, I found myself online, looking up Janice DeWitt's home number.

I curled up in my bed, piled the covers on, and dialed with spaghetti fingers.

Riiiiing.

Riiiiing.

Riiiiing.

C'mon, Nick (GABE!), answer!

Then someone did. "Hello." The raspy, tired voice belonged to Gabe's grandmother. I pictured her crying in that small house all alone. I pictured her crying even more when she found him on her doorstep.

"May I speak to Gabe, please?"

In the silence that followed, I couldn't breathe. Then, "You nosey reporters need to stop calling my grandson! He's got enough to deal with! THANK YOU, NOT!"

And the phone went dead.

I held it for the longest time, feeling numb inside.

I wondered why he hadn't called. I chided myself for being selfish.

CHAPTER TWENTY

The day of the recital, I practiced my solo plus the whole concert three times. I set up the keyboard on my bed, playing hunched over my lap, pretending I was Beethoven—or someone equally tortured.

When I was finished, I drank a glass of apple juice and forced myself to have a peanut butter and jelly sandwich. Like most other foods, this had been off-limits at one time during the course of my post-Dad eating issues, and I was under strict orders to eat something healthy whenever I felt stressed.

For this concert, we were wearing burgundy gowns. "For autumn!" Dr. Fawn had said. I put my gown on at four o'clock and went downstairs, and talked to Mom about the people from the DOD.

"So weird," she said, in the same way she said *weird* when she was talking about me. I nodded and said something I don't remember anymore.

The ride seemed to last forever and take no time at all. It was raining and the Volvo made its old rain noise, a clinking metal sound no one had ever been able to ID. I held my hands in front of the vents and tried to absorb the heat, but when we got into Denver, I was freezing, prompting Mom to ask me, "Have you eaten anything?"

"Yes."

"What kind of thing?"

"A lot of different stuff." I shot her a look that said *Get off it*, and Mom gave me one that said *Are you lying to me, young lady?*

"I'm fine," I told her snippishly. "Just nervous."

For the rest of the ride to Boettcher Hall I thought about Nick—Gabe—*Nick*. How, to me, he would always be Nick. I thought about the day that I had shot him, how warm I'd felt when I looked at him as we walked. I thought about him touching my leg. About the way he looked when he'd said he wanted to turn the TV off anyway. How he had given me that out. How he had hugged me right before he hopped out of the Volvo.

He'd been sitting in this very spot, where I was now. Even driving to his grandma's house, he had seemed…so permanent.

And now he was gone.

And how selfish was I that all I could think about was me, when Gabe was going through heaven knew what, and his family and his friends…

I was no one to him. I needed to quit thinking about him.

The concert went well. I played my solo without any errors—not even the minor, tempo kind. I played like I belonged in an orchestra. Bree came up to me afterward and told me I had done well, and seeing her and her oboe was like a knee right to the chest. I'd given Sara Kate some thought (mainly of the *Hoface is ditching me for Ami* sort), but Bree… Well, I'd forgotten Bree existed in the last few days.

Impulsively, I hugged her. "You did great, too, B."

She smiled, and I was smiling at her when a warm weight dropped onto my shoulder. I turned.

"Nick!"

I didn't mean to say his name (ex-name). It was just like in the movies, where the person does this little gasp, then blurts something in a breathless voice that always sounds contrived.

As soon as I had thrown my arms around Bree, I forgot her again—everything lost in the shock of seeing Nick.

"Gosh, I'm sorry. Gabe."

Before I knew it, I'd thrown my arms around him, too. I was pretty much the opposite of what a nervous high school girl should be. Seeing him again had made me crazy-bold. I squeezed him as hard as I'd been wanting to—a little harder, even, just to let him know I cared. It never crossed my mind that Gabe would be somewhere else, in mind or emotions or whatever. In that second, I was just a girl—not a stranger he'd spent the night with—and Ni—*Gabe!* was just a guy I liked.

I'm embarrassed to say he pulled away first. I was so embarrassed in the moment, it took me a second to notice that he had his hand on my hip; his arm was draped around my waist. To my surprise, he leaned his forehead against my hair for just one second, hugging me one more brief, hard time.

"Milo," he said.

"It's me!" I pulled back, beaming up at him. I giggled like an idiot.

Gabe smiled, and it seemed kind of the same. A little dimmer, maybe. Somehow, he'd moved his arm from around me and I had grabbed his wrist. I didn't remember doing it; I was like a jellyfish, moving with a tide I couldn't see.

"You look...the same, kind of."

"So do you." He grinned, and that second, he really looked the same.

I wanted to ask how he was doing. If he'd remembered anything. I wanted to tell him about the guys that had snooped around our house. I really, really wanted to hug him one more time, and feel those worn-out jeans, that brown and green button-up pressed against me, with Gabe in them. I wanted to touch his soft copper hair. He'd had a headache last I'd seen him. Did he still?

My mouth was disconnected from my brain.

I said, "How are you here?"

"It's this thing you might have heard of. Walking." He raised his eyebrows. "Driving."

"They let you drive?" I blushed at my stupidity, my crassness, but Gabe just shrugged. "Guess they think I won't get lost again."

"Seriously, though, what brought you here?" I couldn't stand the suspense. Especially when he looked down at his shoes—some kind of strange loafers—and then back up into my eyes and said, "What do you think?"

I had no idea. "Do you know someone in the orchestra?"

He laughed. "I do. And she plays beautifully. You didn't tell me that."

I blushed. "But how did you know—"

"Your calendar," he said.

Right. I had a monthly calendar tacked to my wall. Thinking of Nick reading it, remembering it, coming here... It made me feel like melted chocolate.

I smiled shyly.

"So really," I said, stepping closer to the wing of the stage, which was already starting to be cleared. "How're you doing? Anything... well, anything?" I asked.

Gabe shrugged. Same ole Nick (Gabe). "Probably gonna start school soon."

"Really. Wow." He nodded, but not in a wow kind of way. He looked bored. Unhappy. The next question was hard for me to ask, but I forced it out. "Do you remember anything?"

His discomfort was in every little motion: his clenching shoulders, flexing hands. "Not really," he said, looking at the floor. It was shiny, freshly waxed; I could see our reflection in it.

"Well that's okay. I guess. Or not."

He looked at me, and I could tell he was about to spill. He was going to open up.

And then my mom appeared.

"Milo!" she sang, clapping her hands together as she came up behind Nick, who turned around and blinked at her.

"Milo," she repeated. "Who is this?"

"Um, this is my friend Gabe. We met at symphony camp last summer."

He nodded gamely, and he introduced himself as Gabe DeWitt. Mom took up a few minutes of time, and then she pointed to her watch, a pocket watch put on a strap. She took a step away and said, "We need to leave in a few minutes."

When Mom was gone, I said, "I'm sorry."

"Hey, no problem. I should maybe go."

"You sure?" I felt like an idiot for asking. A big, fat, needy idiot.

"I don't want to get you in any trouble."

I forced a smile. "C'mon. We've seen trouble. This is just a few minutes of talking. It can't be that bad."

Nick smiled a little, too.

"I want to know how you are," I said, a bit too earnestly. "How are your friends? Have you still been having headaches?"

I asked that one with meaning. I could tell Nick got it.

"Nothing," he said. He dropped his tone a notch. "I tried it on my grandmother's arthritis, and she's still taking painkillers. Everything's...normal." And, with a weirdly proud expression: "I hear I even have a girlfriend."

I can only assume my face betrayed me, because the next instant, Nick was laughing. "Not that I need one."

I smiled, and it was fake as fake, and before anyone could notice anything, Nick had me behind the curtain, his big hands on my shoulders, his sweet face right there by mine.

"Milo. Thanks."

He kissed me. And the next second, he was gone.

Chapter Twenty-One

Sunday came and went, one long haze where I wore my crappy sweatpants and an old shirt of my dad's and read part of *The Catcher in the Rye* and walked to Dad's marker (where I felt nothing extraordinary, and was disappointed by it). By the time I got home, it was raining—just a stupid little drizzle.

I was never going to see Nick again. I just knew it. Something about the way he'd said my name, and thanks. I wasn't an intuitive genius, but it didn't take one to get that he was saying bye to me.

Maybe even *Bye, and keep my secret, please.*

By dinnertime, I hadn't eaten anything, and Mom was back up at the turbines doing something I hadn't listened well enough to know, so I fixed myself pancakes (another formerly off-limits food) and ate five and then an apple for good measure. I liked apples.

When I started feeling itchy, like jumping jacks would be a perfect way to counteract the pancakes, I made myself eat a chocolate chip cookie. Then I settled on the couch, my phone in hand. Like Nick would call.

I was calling him Nick because it didn't matter, and to me he would never be Gabe. Gabe DeWitt was someone else's friend. Nick had been mine.

For the longest time, I watched The Weather Channel and I wondered why it mattered. Why he mattered. I had friends. I had school. I had music. I didn't need a guy. So why did I feel like I had lost something?

Maybe it was lack of closure. How the whole thing had gone down. First I shot him and I'd thought I had given him amnesia. Then we'd found out what had really happened. Except that had made no sense, and there were other things that somehow made even less sense, and I'd spent a lot of time worrying about who Nick really was. And what he was. It was strange to think, but some of the stuff that he could do—if he was really doing it, he shouldn't have been able to.

Which was probably part of why I couldn't forget him. I couldn't forget the things he'd done, and nor could I explain them. It was driving me crazy—the mystery of it. As I'd learned with Dad, I wasn't a big fan of the unknown.

My rationale made sense, except when I sank back into the couch cushions and shut my eyes, I was feeling his arms around me. Imagining his lips on mine. More than the kiss— I'd finally been kissed!—I relished the other sensations. I liked the weight of his hand on my back. I liked the warmth of his body, the shape of it: so bulky, so much larger than my own. I liked the expression on his face when he looked at me.

About nine, I broke my embargo on the TV news and started desperately searching for Nick stories. I started calling him Gabe again and promised God that if Gabe and I could keep in touch, I'd be a good friend to him. It didn't have to be anything romantic.

I admitted to myself that maybe I was missing Gabe so much because S.K., Bree, Halah, and I were spinning in such separate orbits. Then I admitted maybe that wasn't the whole reason.

It was 10 when my mom texted and said that Turbine Three was down again. At 10:30, I drifted to sleep—my bleary eyes fixed on the news, still awaiting a story about Gabe.

The revving thunder of a motorcycle brought me out of my dream and back into the living room. Years after my dad had sold his first bike—an old Harley FXR he'd called The Hoss—and moved onto more sophisticated, more expensive bikes, the sound of an approaching Hog still made my chest clench.

I pushed myself up on my elbows, glancing at the one-handed clock above our mantel as I followed the sound down our driveway.

It was only 11:21 p.m., so not unthinkable that someone would be dropping by. I shoved my blanket off and stood, stretching till my muscles ached. It was probably one of Mom's technicians, confused about how to get up to the turbines at night.

By the time I made it to the kitchen window, the best one for scoping out the driveway, the bike and its rider had gone behind the house. I rubbed my eyes and headed back into the den, where a window on the side of the house could give me a view of the backyard if I craned my neck just right.

With the turbines on the mountainside as they were, it surprised me that anyone ever came to our house, but sometimes techs did. Half the time, the distance down our driveway was enough to help them see the flashing lights and realize they'd missed their mark. The other half, they wound up at our door.

I was wondering what kind of dummy could fix a broken turbine but couldn't see a bunch of them perched on the side of a mountain, when I heard a crashing sound in my bedroom, followed by my name.

My blood froze.

"Milo?"

The voice was Nick's.

He sounded hoarse.

All I could think as I ran up the stairs was that he had remembered. He had remembered the wreck, and he had come to my house. His name was Gabe, I reminded myself as I topped the stairs. His name was Gabe—and he had come to my house.

I found him standing in the doorway of my room, wearing ripped jeans and a shredded grey Polo shirt.

In a millisecond, I knew something was wrong. His face was twisted, those brown eyes wide as he panted.

"Milo. I… *Shit*, I'm sorry."

He covered his eyes with his hands for a second, then brushed his fingers through his already messy hair. His right arm was noticeably stiffer; I looked closer and saw that his wrist was swollen, dappled black and blue. I could tell by the stiff set of his shoulder that it hurt to move.

"What's going on?"

He looked at me, his face a mask of angst. He groaned, and rubbed his palm back through his hair. "I shouldn't have come here, but I didn't know where else to go." He inhaled deeply, shoulders rising. "I was at the hospital all day for tests, and when I left, I thought someone had followed me, so I went to the library to lose them but when I came out they grabbed me—"

"Who!"

"These guys in suits. Black guy and white guy. One of them hit me—" he rolled his right shoulder— "and I ended up in an SUV. I fought them and I—" He took a deep breath. "I got out. When I landed..." He glanced at the porch door. "I took someone's bike."

"A Harley," I said stupidly.

And felt stupid for thinking about how stupid I sounded.

Gabe hung his head. "I'm sorry, Milo."

My mind raced, so it was hard for me to think of what to say. Men in black suits, a SUV... I could feel my body start to buzz.

"Don't be sorry. There's nothing to be sorry for, okay? I'm glad you came. Sit down." He cast a dubious glance at his jeans—ripped down one side, I realized now, from his scuffle with the road—but I put my hand on the curve of his back, pressing lightly. "You sit down on the bed, and I'm gonna get my phone and—"

"No!" he cried. And softer: "Please don't get your phone."

"Okay, I won't. I won't call anyone. Okay?"

He nodded, and the guilt was back. "Milo," he said, "I think I lost them, but... I'm not sure. I shouldn't have come here. I can't believe I did."

"It's okay. Come here..." I tried to be gentle as I wrapped my hand around his good elbow and led him to the bed. "Sit. Wait. I'm gonna go to the bathroom and get a few things, and then we're gonna split."

I rifled through my cabinets and raced back into my room with my battered Easter basket full of first aid stuff. As I crossed the rug, Gabe looked down at the mattress and half jumped, half toppled off the bed.

"What?!"

I got close enough to see: His blue jeans, on the right side, by his hip, were stained crimson.

He pulled up his shirt. Through the mangled fibers of the denim, I could see torn flesh.

"Holy crap. That's bad. Really bad."

He grunted.

"Just...take those off—or pull them down. We need to clean that."

He looked up, like he was just remembering I was there. "I don't need to. It's okay."

"Yes you do, and no it's not."

I don't know why I didn't tell him about Sid and Diego. If I had, Nick might have actually gotten away.

I guess at that point I just didn't want to be left behind.

CHAPTER TWENTY-TWO

He still tried to leave. Tried to stand up, said he needed to move.

"Are you insane?!" I grabbed his good hand. Now that I'd seen the gash on his hip, I wasn't letting him go anywhere. "Sit down! I have to bandage that. Then we'll go." This time, I helped him back onto the bed, propped a pillow on his lap and helped him move his arm onto it. "Don't worry about getting blood on my sheets. They're old."

"That's not what I'm worried about. If they come—"

"Wouldn't they already be here by now?"

We were both quiet for a moment—both straining our ears. "See?"

I rifled through my stuff, found an old bottle of Hyrdocodone—from when I'd gotten my wisdom teeth removed—and shook one out into my palm. "First things first." I held it out. "Painkillers."

His teeth were clenched. "I don't need one."

"Take one for me?"

He shook his head. Another deep breath, accompanied by a longsuffering look I would never have put on Nick's smooth face. He opened his mouth like he was going to say something—probably apologize—but then he closed it. A second later, his face twisted in a look that made me blush. "You're too good, Milo."

I was glowing like Rudolph's nose. I could feel it. I pulled my hair around, over my blotchy chest and neck, and I tried to look busy putting the cap back on the bottle.

"I'm not this nice to everybody."

When I finally dared to look at Gabe, he was looking at me, too.

I felt like someone in a movie as he raised his left hand and touched the ends of my hair. When he lowered it, he looked sad, but in a way that made my stomach flutter.

"You can put the pill back. I don't want it."

"You need to take at least a half. It doesn't do anything major. Trust me. It was worthless for my wisdom teeth."

I grabbed a canteen from my nightstand and held it out to him, along with the pill. He looked at my windows, and I put my hand on his knee. "If they were on you, they'd be here by now. Remember?"

When he still didn't take it, I ran my pointer finger very gently over the puffy skin of his wrist, and Gabe's body tensed.

"See?" I pulled away.

He broke the pill in two and swallowed one half.

"If they come," he said, as I grabbed a roll of gauze, "I'll run, you stay here."

No way in a million years was that the plan, but I figured why argue.

"They won't." I stood. "BRB. I've gotta go downstairs and get you an icepack."

I checked the windows on the first floor, my stomach in a large knot. When I saw no headlights, I grabbed an ice pack and a soft, clean rag and dashed back up the stairs.

Gabe sat, still and quiet, as I wrapped his wrist with gauze.

"Do you feel like talking about it?"

He sighed, and I handed him the ice pack, which he draped carefully around his wrist.

"You know, we did this backwards," I muttered. "I should have had you help me with your pants, and then we should have put the ice on your arm."

Without a word, Gabe rolled onto his side, used his good arm to unbutton his fly, and hiked his jeans down, giving me access to his hip—and a blush-inducing amount of skin.

But the sexy was ruined by his hip, bruised and scraped and swollen like the wrist. "Oh, Gabe."

"'S not Gabe."

I dabbed a gauze square in alcohol and hovered over his hip. "Hold your breath, okay?"

But as I cleaned the cut, he talked through gritted teeth. "I'm not him. I feel…nothing for them. My grandmother, my 'friends.'" Those brown eyes flickered up to me. "It's not like with you."

It was wrong to feel so glad, I told myself. Wrong for me to think 'he likes me.'

I dragged the alcohol over his flayed skin, then dared lean close to blow it dry. I felt his hand come down on my shoulder, and was surprised to feel him leaning on me.

"I'm not a normal person," he said softly, to my hair.

"Why not?"

His laugh sounded more like a croak. "Where to start? I'm awesome at basketball."

"And that's weird how?"

"Because Gabe never played basketball, yet somehow I shot 322 of 322 at the YMCA. I only stopped because people were starting to notice."

I whistled, though at that point I'd seen weirder from him.

He must have been able to tell I wasn't impressed, because he said, "I can play the piano. I can play anything I hear by ear, and I can play it perfectly the first time."

My mouth hung open.

Nick grimaced. "I've never missed a single question on Jeopardy. And Grandma DeWitt watches a lot of Jeopardy."

"How—"

"To top it all off, I'm not going to remember anything."

"They told you that?" I made my fingers move, gently taping gauze to his hip, but I felt sick with sorrow for him. "The doctors, at University Hospital?"

I tried to focus on those doctors as I folded his boxer shorts gently over the wound. When I was done, I rocked back on my heels. "Why do they think that?"

"No brain injury."

I nodded, like that meant something, and Nick grew more animated.

"I know everything in all my textbooks. And you know how I escaped?" I shook my head. "I made the wheel lock up. The steering wheel. From the back of the van. And then I made the doors unlock. I pressed the break a little bit, and I jumped out."

I shook my head, not getting it. "How did you—"

"I just did! The same way I stole the motorcycle. I wanted it to go, and it just did! That's how I fixed your dad's bike, too. I just didn't tell you."

I thought about the TV, and I felt chills.

"I've still been getting headaches," he continued. "All the time. But it's usually when I think of certain things. Like iron. Or water. I know the exact conductivity of my grandmother's jewelry. Platinum, gold, silver. When I walk outside, sometimes I can feel the angle that the Earth is tilted. I have this sense of where we are…around the sun. And pills," he said. "I understand them. What they're made of." He took a deep breath, like he was preparing to jump into an icy pond, and said, "I remember the crash. I remember looking at it from above."

My mouth dropped. "Did you see yourself?"

"It wasn't me. I can't explain it," he said, reaching up to push his hair back.

I noticed a scratch on the back of his neck as he moved.

"You've got another scrape."

He looked down at his lap, like he knew I was changing the subject, and he was frustrated. I didn't know what to say, or what to think. What he was claiming was impossible. But so was bringing people back to life.

I couldn't deal with it, so I focused on what I could. "Why don't you roll over? Stretch out on the bed and let me clean your neck?"

Frowning deeply—obviously upset—he started to get up.

I caught him by the chest, my fingers tangling in his shirt. "Please?"

With a long look at my face, Nick turned slowly, easing himself down on his good elbow. He rested his right arm above his head, and I stared at his back, thinking how beautiful he was, how strange.

Then I stretched out beside him, finding the sore spot with my fingertips and gauze.

Chapter Twenty-Three

I shouldn't have come to Milo's house, but I was riding for my life, and when I thought about it ending, all I'd wanted—literally the only thing I thought about—was her.

It was startling, the clarity, the sense of purpose, because shortly after I saw Milo's concert, I got mind-jacked. I didn't know by what, but the presence had a serious hard-on for calculus and physics, other things I shouldn't know or care about. I had a freaky suspicion that it was the Real Me, and that the Real Me was some kind of wizard/astrophysicist.

I spent two days in my bed after it happened, hung over on numbers, figures, but by the third day I could handle it. And my superpower had come back, stronger.

I knew intuitively how to control the van, how many meters away the Harley was when I landed, how to start it, how to control it.

I ran for it as the van spun, tires screeching as it turned to come back for me. It had been modified, was faster than the bike, but I knew the town grid completely, and I'd clogged their fuel injector, which meant that ten minutes after our little chase started, I had lost them.

I doubled back, took an indirect path to get to Milo's house. I didn't want to leave an easy trail. When I pulled up and they were nowhere to be seen, I thought I had evaded them, told myself I had gotten away. But it wasn't until I saw Milo that I realized what I'd done. I should have added to my lead, driven far away, stolen another bike, a car, hopped a train, gone anywhere but where I was. Where she was.

And what did I get for my utter stupidity?

Milo, wide-eyed and concerned. Milo, rubbing my back, tapping my knee. Milo heedless of the danger. Milo, achingly close.

She was leaning over me now, blowing on the scrape she'd just cleaned. "That feel any better?"

I nodded, my nose and forehead digging into her blankets.

"Good." I felt her hand trail up my spine, then lift away and land atop my hair.

"You can go to sleep, you know. I'll keep watch, just in case."

I shook my head, dizzy from the pill and her soft hand. "I need to... leave..."

Voices. Thousands, millions, billions humming in my head, in the same tones, so there was no way to divide them, and no need to.

They were all one thing. Voices from one rattled mind. The chorus that made me.

I had the horrible sensation, as I lay there listening to them, that I wasn't real.

I shook my head, because I was. I was Nick. And my true self was close, floating just out of my reach. Along with something else. Something I didn't want to know.

Something that had to do with Milo.

And suddenly I knew that we were talking about Milo. The voices were vibrating her name. I had shared something I shouldn't have. I'd revealed something forbidden.

While some part of me continued lying on Milo's bed, the rest of me was taken somewhere else: a place I couldn't see clearly, but somewhere big—a vast ballroom. Unlike last time, where the space I was in had felt so small and crowded, this place was huge and dark. There were others here; I could feel them, but I couldn't place them.

I didn't want to. I was angry.

An error was being made. A wrong, multiplying. If it continued on this way, if *we* kept on this way, we would fragment.

This was imparted, but present me didn't understand. I didn't want to. Already I was beginning to form *I*, to forsake *we*.

Maybe we should sever ties right now. Because if it happened by accident or famine...

A deafening voice cut through my thoughts, more intention than sound, pushing me out of awareness.

It was over as soon as it had begun. Maybe sooner. This time I didn't moan or even writhe, but the pain was still crushing. I arched my back and tried to bring my hands to my skull, which felt like it was being ripped apart. Milo said something. I felt her hands on me. I felt another sudden wave of sensation—like if I wanted to, I could go back to the place where... I didn't understand what it was... I didn't want to, so I shut my mind off. After a minute of nothing but soft panting, I was able to hear Milo.

"Nick? Nick, are you alright?" she murmured near my ear.

The way I saw it, I was pretty well screwed. Not to mention that my head hurt like God's hands were boxing my ears.

"Nick?" She shook me slightly. "Are you asleep? I'm sorry to bother you, but you're breathing kind of funny."

I nodded—so much effort. "I'm…sleeping," I said into her sheets.

And then I was.

CHAPTER TWENTY-FOUR

Watching Nick sleep was like nothing I had done before. Well, obviously. But really, it was...incredible. Before that night, when I wrapped Nick's warm, sleeping body in my blankets and snuggled up next to him, I'd never felt like I was missing all that much. I'd never been on the romantic fast-track like Halah, and unlike S.K., who said she was saving her virginity for Chris Pine, I'd never thought about my own—or even making it through the first few bases. If I was honest, those things scared me.

But lying beside Nick—*just* lying—was something I decided I could quickly get used to. I closed my eyes and felt the warmth of him. I closed my eyes and felt overwhelmed by how much I cared for him.

We were only friends, of course, but it was pretty clear I liked him more than that. I didn't think of him in terms of "boyfriend," probably because our situation was so weird, but when I lay there by him, my heart felt like a balloon bobbing on a string.

After a long time, he turned to me and wrapped one arm around my waist, and my face ended up on his chest, where I could smell his guy-ish scent, plus soap or cologne—something clean, like a mountain brook.

I couldn't sleep—or wouldn't sleep—so I thought about everything he'd told me. It should have been difficult to believe, but it wasn't. Starting with that whistle—that stupid little metal whistle—scalding my leg, and going all the way up until the party, when I hadn't felt Annabelle's pulse, and Nick had brought it back, I'd seen first-hand that Nick was special. And I figured that when you saw things for yourself, you didn't really have a choice but to believe.

I had extracted myself from his grasp—as painful as it was—to go to the bathroom (leaving a pillow behind to hold my spot) when I heard the doorbell ring. I froze, hand on the bathroom doorknob, desperately hoping I'd imagined it.

It rang again, two quick dings, and I knew who it was. My chest went cold, the rest of me still. I wasn't panicked. I was focused.

I crept down the stairs, my body tight and hard, ready for action. Mom slept with her fan on, and she didn't have Dad's ears. I peeked out the windows in the library, on the middle floor, by her and Dad's room, and I saw the big, dark SUV.

The doorbell rang again, followed by someone's fist pounding the door. A second later Mom flew out of her room like a bat out of a cave, so when her footsteps hit the stairs, I jumped a mile. My instinct was to run to Nick, but I followed her down, waiting on the stairs while she answered the door in her same, clear, wide-awake Mom voice. I heard a crisp, rich voice: Sid's. When I crept down to the bottom of the stairs, I caught a glimpse of him and a pretty, short-haired blonde who introduced herself as Ursula.

"Mrs. Mitchell," the girl said, "is your daughter home?"

I jerked like I'd been shot, then whirled and ran upstairs. My room was empty. I ran onto the roof, where I found Nick heading down the stairs. He turned to me, hard-eyed.

"Milo, go inside."

"No way."

"I mean it, Milo." And when I shook my head: "Please."

I meant to be reasonable, to be rational, because clearly I was already too involved to make my staying worth anything. But panic finally found me, and I launched myself at him. "I'm going with you," I declared as my hands clenched his shirt.

Nick shook me off and darted down the stairs, and I followed. As he headed for the Harley, parked below the deck and hidden by some bushes, I grabbed his arm and pulled him toward Dad's Agusta.

"Milo, please. I don't want you hurt."

"Forget about it," I said. "I'm coming."

He jumped onto the bike like he thought he could lose me, but I was faster than I looked.

"Damnit, Milo!"

I locked my arms around his waist and we were off, tearing down the driveway, whipping through the grass as Nick cut across the yard toward Mitchell Road.

We could make it, I thought, as the dark billowed around us. We could make it because we had a lead.

For a good five seconds, I embraced this fantasy. As Nick swerved onto Mitchell Road and we whizzed underneath the turbines, spinning, flashing against the pink-gray of the clouds.

Then I heard a noise from Nick that sounded like a curse. I leaned around him, and I realized: We were riding toward two motorcycles. Or rather, they were riding toward us. Their drivers must have been armed with guns, because as they sped by us, I felt something graze the sole of my shoe; my heel felt hot and stung a little. I screamed, and Nick sped up, and all too soon they had spun around and were behind us, and the noise of three bikes at max speed was roaring through my head, and my heart was beating so quickly I thought it might explode.

"Take a right!" I said, too late; he'd already done it. We tilted so sharply I swear I felt my leg brush gravel, and I said, "Go straight! I know a place!"

For just a second, just one blissful fraction of a moment, we pulled out ahead; I wondered if he was doing something to their bikes. The next minute they were gaining again, their motorcycles faster than the Agusta.

I clutched Nick harder, glanced behind.

Oh dear God, they were closer! They would ram us, knock us off our bike; they would shoot us.

Out of nowhere I remembered an old obstacle course, a place up to our right—unless we'd passed it; had we passed it?—where Halah and I had gone two summers before to watch some boy she'd liked jump dirt bikes. I remembered that the course was in a clearing, facing a road that wound toward S.K.'s family's cabin. The cabin was the only place I knew, and it was really isolated, because S.K.'s dad was part doctor, part philosopher, and he had this thing about *Walden* and—shit, the turnoff!

"Nick, TURN LEFT!"

Either I was loud or he had supernatural ears, 'cause Nick pulled hard to the left, the back tire spun and we fishtailed, and I screamed and thought we would skid. But Nick was like a pro, and we were shooting through the woods. Our pursuer shot past, unable to turn, and then we were in the clearing and the moon lit the ramps and without me telling him, Nick took one of them—a large one that shot us high into the air, so high that the force of our landing took my breath away. My arms lost their hold on Nick, but gravity slammed me into his back and as we shot off, I somehow caught his belt loop and I managed to call, "RIGHT THERE!"

Right there, between two stones, there was the little path that led us to the road. And by the time we made it to the road, no one was behind us.

This lasted maybe ten seconds, then the bikes were back. No, *bike*. Turning around—so dizzy; I might fall—I saw only one headlight and I wanted to cheer even though I was frozen with terror.

Somehow we kept ahead of the bike as we started traveling up, taking turns at terrifying speed. But we never got ahead.

Then I felt Nick's torso start to tremble, and again, I thought that we were going to wreck. The last thing I thought before we left the ground was that I couldn't blame him if he killed us. He'd done so well, and he wasn't a stunt man or an angel or a vampire. He was just a guy who did weird things.

I opened my eyes, and we were flying off a cliff. I noticed the railing of a lookout point and thought *ironic*. This was how Nick had died before—if he was Gabe, if he had died—and we were going to—

"Oof!"

We hit the ground hard, quicker than if we had fallen all the way. The bike bounced so low my shoes touched the ground; the impact shimmied up my shins and thighs, exploding in pain that wrapped my waist. I screamed, and Nick fell forward, over the handles, and the bike tipped sideways, landing on our legs, and in that second, I heard a powerful roar somewhere above us.

It took me a moment to realize we were on an overhang. Nick had overshot the road and sped through Johnson's Post, a popular lookout point, and somehow we had made it to a ledge that hung beneath it.

And more important, we had lost our tail.

Chapter Twenty-Five

The valley was bathed in soft moonlight, as if the craggy peaks and sparkling suburbs below were behind a sheet of wax paper. It took me several seconds to notice I was leaning sideways, my left leg pinned under the hot weight of the Agusta, my forehead jammed into Nick's back. He groaned and pushed the bike off of us, balancing it between his legs and leaning forward, onto the handlebars.

"Nick," I said, wobbly. "Are you okay?"

He was panting, but he quickly turned and reached for me. His warm hand touched down on my hair, a rough, worried caress. "Are you?"

"I think so."

Still clutching his waist, I looked over my shoulder at the iron rail that framed the cement lookout point. Dust billowed from the rocky path that curved into the brush beside it. It wasn't an official trail, just a path made by vacationers too adventurous for the same snapshot everyone else got.

"Hop off," he told me gruffly, then maneuvered his own weight off the bike and held out his good hand for me. Working mostly with that arm and limping slightly, he pulled the bike toward the rock wall, making us invisible from the road.

Before I could even move to help him, he'd cut its lights and captured my hand. His fingers laced with mine—surprisingly intimate—and he gave my hand a warm, tight squeeze. He exhaled deeply, his breath a cold cloud that floated toward the stars.

My heart was pounding. My knees were shaking. But the truth is, I loved standing there with him, having just escaped something terrible. I felt completely exhilarated.

He grabbed my other hand and turned me to face him—imploring with his eyes. "Milo, you shouldn't have come with me."

I was still scared and I didn't like the tension on his face, but I was also rocking the adrenaline. I laughed. "Nick, we got away. Was that an accident?" I asked, glancing at the crumbly path behind us.

He shrugged, the motion making our linked hands swing. "I knew it was there."

I opened my mouth to ask him how, and he jerked in another breath. "I think I've seen it before." He nodded up toward the sky, and I said, *"Oh."*

Pike's Peak was somewhere above us, farther up the winding mountain road. If Nick remembered anything from the accident—*If Nick had* been *in the accident…*

My legs still trembled, so I turned my gaze to them, to the pebbly floor of rock below my feet. The ledge we'd landed on was fairly large as far as terrifying mountainside ledges went—15 feet by 10, I guesstimated—and the front tire of the bike had landed a mere two feet from its edge. Just a nudge, and we'd be vulture-food.

I glanced up at Nick, whose hands still had my own. With his Polo stretched across his wide shoulders, still rising and falling with his heavy breaths, and his hair wind-whipped around his dirt-smudged face, he looked like a cross between a warrior and a model for Ralph Lauren.

"That was…amazing," I said.

He didn't seem to share my enthusiasm.

"Who are those guys?" I wondered. "What do they want with you?" If they were willing to risk killing two teenagers…

Nick's shrug was more a jerk. "I don't know what they want. I've got some ideas but…" He shook his head, like he was trying to shake the dirt out of his hair. "You really shouldn't be here. I don't know how to escape them. The Department of Defense?" His eyes bored into mine. "I don't know how to keep you safe."

"You don't have to do anything. It was my choice."

"I can take you home," he offered. "You could tell your mom I forced you to come."

Now it was my turn to laugh. "Don't be insane. I'd never do that." I squeezed his hands for emphasis.

"Then you're risking your life. You get that, don't you?"

I hadn't, actually. Not until that gaze drilled into me. As the realization permeated, I was surprised to find I hardly cared. When I was with Nick, on a cliff, in a costume shop, even in my room, I felt, as cheesy and cliché as it sounds, alive. And happy to be.

So when he said, "*Milo*," I said, "Nick." I looked into his eyes, so dark and pure, and I said, "I've got a place that we can go."

And so, together, we turned the bike around and got it up the path. Nick revved us off into the night, headed for Sara Kate's cabin—and I prayed Dr. Mackris was Thoreau enough to keep it off the map.

We passed Pike's Peak, and I started to hallucinate—or dream. I tried to focus on the double yellow lines, but they flashed in and out, like we were moving through a series of pictures.

I thought it was the pain: It streaked down my neck, across my shoulders, up into my head until my eyes felt like they might pop out.

I adjusted my grip on the bike's handlebars, but my fingers felt weak and useless.

I turned my focus to Milo, a blanket of soft heat on my back. Her hair flapped in the wind, tickling my neck. Her arms twined around my waist, comforting, familiar. Gritting my teeth until my jaw ached, I mastered my body, but then my mind floated up like a balloon.

I watched the road and steered the bike, but other images overlaid the mountain scenery. I saw a maroon Honda Odyssey sailing through a metal rail and plunging, in slow motion, toward the cliffs. There was a moment where I felt a bite of urgency: a remembered sensation that beckoned, promising revelation if I...

I grabbed one of Milo's hands and guided it to the handlebar. I was zoning out. I just couldn't help it anymore.

I felt vast and deep, more valley than person. It was true, I sensed: I didn't have a body. Even without one, I was processing data. Digesting details. I saw a storm of sparks glowing gold and silver. Like a puff of smoke, I forced myself toward them, trying to catch them. They moved so fast they streaked together. Trying to follow made me feel stretched like taffy.

Somewhere very far away, I was moaning and clutching my head. I heard Milo's voice…

But I was somewhere else.

I was something else. Not I, but *we*. There was no singularity. And yet, I was created. I was made separate. Not because I endorsed the logic of division, but because I *wanted*, and the nature of the desire made me.

Something played at the edges of my memory, something that tugged me, like a string attached to my center. It was heavy—I could feel the awful weight of it, and I didn't dare go near it. I pulled away, back to the bike and back to Milo.

My head cleared enough for me to see that we'd turned onto another road—a thin, gravel road. I was hunched over, mostly limp but still hanging onto the handlebars. Milo was wrapped around me like a coat, scooted so close that I could feel her frantic breaths. Her chest pressed to my back. Her hands curled over mine. I straightened up, and she startled.

"Nick! Omigod, are you okay?!"

I glanced back at her, found her face twisted with concern. I tried to nod and felt her squeeze my hands.

For some amount of time—*eight minutes and eleven seconds*—we drove like that, with Milo's hands on mine, traveling slowly. Then she tapped my arm, and I realized that the rocks ahead were partially obscuring a tall, wood fence. With painstaking effort, I compressed the brakes, and Milo hopped off.

She had the gate open in no time. Or maybe it took a while. At some point we passed through it, and I felt good knowing we were safe. Or she was.

I would leave before they found her. That was the last thought that I had before the pain was back, lighting up my mind, and the string inside me was pulled taut.

CHAPTER TWENTY-SIX

I guided the bike into the Mackris' dark carport and cut the power. An automatic light blinked on, and I saw that Nick was half slumped over, holding his head.

When I squeezed his shoulder, he muttered something, then sort of jumped away from my hand, like he wasn't sure who I was or where we were.

"Are you okay?" What a stupid question. I pressed my palm onto his cheek and found it warm. "Do you think it's from where they hit you on the head?"

Nick just blinked at me, and when I hopped off the bike and held out my hands to help him off, he blinked some more, reminding me of my favorite animal, an owl—except it wasn't cute. He had circles under his eyes, and his black pupils had eaten up the gentle brown of his irises.

"Come on and we'll go inside." I rubbed his shoulder, worried that shaking him or getting in his face would make him worse.

He flicked his dazed eyes up at me, then tried to throw one leg over the bike. His foot caught the seat somehow, and the next second, both Nick and the Agusta were crashing into the small staircase that led up to the cabin's side door.

Nick caught himself—but with the wrong hand. As his

wrist folded back, he let out an awful howl. By the time I lifted the bike off, he was lying flat against the concrete, one fist in his hair, his bad arm lying limp and purple—fingers flexed.

"Nick?"

He moaned and I knelt beside him, my hand hovering over his hair, wanting to soothe but too afraid to touch him.

"Nick?"

His eyes opened, found mine, and he held out his good hand. I took it for a second, then threaded one arm around his waist and helped him up the stairs. The Mackrises kept a spare key inside the mouth of a little frog statue beside the mat. As I worried how I would get it without dropping Nick, he braced his arm against the wall.

"Just a sec." I let go of him and bent to grab the key, praying S.K.'s family hadn't installed a security system since I'd been here the previous fall.

I unlocked the door and we moved into the mudroom, where I found myself facing the familiar sight of a stacked washer-dryer and a pile of fragrant firewood.

I helped Nick through the huge kitchen, to an L-shaped beige suede couch that framed a flatscreen and a coffee table. He fell back on it and covered his forehead with his elbow, then hoarsely mumbled, "Sorry, Milo."

"It's okay. We're safe here." I wasn't sure that it was true, but I wanted him relaxed. A soft sigh came from his lips, and Nick held out his hand.

I wrapped it in mine, sinking to the rug as a helicopter thrummed somewhere nearby.

It was like a dream. Maybe it was a dream. My wrenching headache was gone, leaving me light and empty. I was somewhere indefinable, somewhere vast and pale; nothing existed but sensation.

The backdrop for all other thought was this: something must be found to save us. This was a driving urgency: we were all in trouble, the end was nearing quickly, and the intention identified now as I had to...What?

I wasn't alone. It was something we were doing. Conserving. Seeking. Exploring.

Though the empty space rolled out endlessly around me, I had the sense that I was situated somewhere smaller, and within my immediate area, I was not alone. I was never alone. I didn't think to wonder who the others were or to question my relation to them. Those questions needed no answers. It was as it had always been.

I looked ahead and saw waves. Vibrations. I knew they were language, and somehow, I understood.

Energy. We were running out of energy. To my surprise, I told the group that I had a solution.

Look.

A real-time, multidimensional model of a blue planet appeared, drawn with my piece of the mind. I felt a pang of longing, saw a magnified image of the light I had colored orange. I pushed it down inside me—hidden, safe.

I paced the rug. Nick was out. He'd been muttering for the last half hour, nonsense words and sounds that made my throat tight. As I paced the colorful woven rug, my mind was a whirlwind of fear and worry.

Who—what—was Nick? My suspicion that he was *something* was confirmed, had been confirmed when I'd first seen the men from the Department of Defense. I thought about crazy things. That TV show, *Heroes*. I thought about *X-Men* and *The Bourne Identity* and that ancient, cheesy show, *Touched by an Angel*. Looking down at Nick, so pale and still, I wondered if he was strong enough to be okay despite whatever was happening to him.

I sat down on the round, wood coffee table, wanting to take Nick's hand but somehow unable to make myself reach out for him.

I stood up, walked to the window, looked out. It was isolated up here, nothing but darkness, with fuzzy shapes I knew were trees and blocks of darker dark against the satiny black sky: jagged peaks with snow on top. S.K.'s dad had done a good job finding isolation.

I'd heard a few more helicopters in the time Nick had been muttering, but almost as soon as I heard them, they were gone. Once I saw what I was sure was a spot light, in the distance.

What would they do if they found us? What would they do to Nick? Badly as I hated to admit it, I had the idea that I, at least, would be excused from this somehow. That I could play the clueless girl card I normally hated, and I could save my gutless neck if I had to. But they were *after* Nick—and *why*?

I slid back down beside him, on the rug, taking his hand in mine. I spread my palm out on his cheek and found it warm as last time I had checked.

He murmured something about "female," and then shook his head, and I said, "Shhh." I stroked his soft, thick hair. "Shh, it's okay." And then I added: "Gabe."

I wanted to see if he responded to the name, but he didn't move.

"Nick," I said instead. "Nick, it's Milo."

I wondered where the feds were looking, how long it would take them to look here.

"Nick, it's Milo. Wake up, please?"

Nick writhed, and he opened his eyes and said my name.

They shut again before I could answer, and he was back to dreamland.

I had, in my head, the number of her weight, in grams, down to the seventh decimal. I knew her mass and the shapes of all her cells. I knew her age in seconds, the paths her mind took when she was thinking, her feelings. I knew her location, too.

Golden, Colorado, United States of America. Latitude and longitude: N 39° 45' 20.2746", W 105° 13' 15.9954". Such a strange measurement system... Everything about this place so very strange.

So far away. But I had reason to go there.

"Nick?" I shook his arm. "Nick! Wake up!" I inhaled deeply, slapped his cheek. "Wake up! You've gotta wake up, NOW!"

177

The helicopters roared nearby, and they were getting louder.

CHAPTER TWENTY-SEVEN

From out of the void that was my holding place, a cyclone started turning. I sensed it as one might see it— suddenly there, building momentum fast, growing larger and larger. There is a difference, though; a cyclone destroys; I was engulfed. My void took other things into itself, made them itself.

I had the sense, also, of sound. Of something roaring.

I felt the steam-roll of energy. A heavy, heavy vat of knowledge. Of expectation. I relaxed—"closed my eyes"— and after resisting it for so long, finally gave myself to it.

There is no way to accurately describe our existence in human words. No way to describe the translation of material that occurs when switching forms—from one of Us, to human. From human ("Nick") to a part of Us.

Because with us, there is no *one*. We are joined at our core: one strong white rib in a long and curving chest, one small cell dividing alongside countless others. Some blink on while others fade away. We function as an army—one. And within one, segments too attached to truly be called individual.

Still, I have taught myself to simplify. To slough off all the rest, to find the thin, bleak light inside the flame and carry it away. I have my own mind; this knowledge calls to me through time. Through space.

I, Me, One—I know my mission, what I need to find. I needed Milo, too, but in the way of two things merging into one.

I needed Milo, and I found her.

I opened my eyes and I saw her face and I felt like it was mine. Milo was a part of me, and I a part of her, and this was something We did poorly; though conjoined, We lacked the desire to be one.

Desire had been abandoned, with ego, pride, self-interest.

Or had it?

"Nick," her lips said—minus sound. I felt her hands on my warm cheeks and saw my mission's goal.

Gold.

It was why I'd come here.

We needed gold to function. Without it, we would cease to transmit.

I felt a punch in the back of my head, and my eyes snapped open.

There were lights outside. I could see shadows moving through them, figures on ropes, dangling like spiders from a web.

I was awake and I was Me. Not Nick or Gabe DeWitt,

but Me. I remembered. I understood. And now I knew why they were coming for me, what they wanted. I knew, too, that they would never get it.

They didn't have the power I had. No human came close.

I stood and raised my arms. I could feel them outside, the men already on the ground, surrounding the cabin. And more coming, dangling from their lines. With only a thought, I made the cabin's wood walls bulge. With another, boards were pushed out of place, shattered under the pressure of my will, exploding out so thousands of splinters ripped our would-be captors to shreds. I shut my eyes, applied some force, and sent the choppers spiraling. I felt the cyclone I'd created, heard their depthless boom against the mountains.

When it was done, I lowered my tingling fingers and turned, very slowly, to face Milo. Her mouth was open. Her eyes were wide. She hugged herself and backed away.

CHAPTER TWENTY-EIGHT

I'd known he wasn't normal. Even thought he wasn't human. I'd seen the evidence—seen him bring somebody back from the dead! But when Nick made the cabin explode, made the helicopters crash like kids' toys, I was finally afraid of him. Only one wall stood—the one behind me—and through the trees, across the cliffs, I could see fires where the helicopters burned.

I backed against the wall instinctively—cornered prey. The wolf in front of me was panting, pale and weak, but it wasn't enough to make me safe from him. He turned to me, and my heart stopped.

"I remembered," he said, soft and low. "I'm not Gabe. Gabe died. I... borrowed his body."

I was breathing harder than he was then. Trying to.

"I don't... get it."

I didn't want to get it. I didn't want any of this to be happening. Milo's Great Adventure had become a nightmare.

And it got worse. "This is not my world."

The look on his face, the sadness in his voice—it seemed fake. Everything about this moment seemed unreal. As I thought that, something in the distance boomed; a helicopter exploding. I jumped, cried, "What the hell are you talking about?"

His eyes flitted skyward, toward the stars scattered above, and in a low and wistful voice he said, "This planet is not my planet."

The hits kept coming.

"That's crazy!" My voice cracked. I felt outraged. Insane.

And the wilder I felt, the calmer Nick appeared. His body still trembled, but the inner core of him was pure, hard steel. "Milo. I'm not human."

I gasped—a hiccup-gasp, a sort of laugh. The sound that crazy people make. "Are you saying you're an *alien*?"

A small wince, and one word: "Yeah."

I started cackling. He just watched me, and in the stillness of his gaze I noticed something new. Something that hadn't been there before. Something that changed him.

I clenched my jaw. I clenched my jaw until it ached. And when I spoke again, I sounded furious. "So you're an *alien*? What the hell?!"

"I'm sorry." He looked ashamed. I had to fight the urge to slap his face.

"You're kidding me. You're kidding, right?"

"No. Milo—"

"Stop it!" I backed up, bumping the wall. I held up my hands. "Don't tell me that! Be quiet!"

He was saying something, but I didn't hear him. I was walking backward. Tripping, getting up. Past the wall. The one wall he'd left standing.

I was into what had been the back yard of the cabin, stopped between two bushes that bloomed pink in spring. Nick had followed me, was within touching distance, and he had his arm out, like maybe he was going to touch me. I made a strangled, screaming sound—Just a burst of noise, because I was nothing compared to him, and it shook me to my core.

Gradually, through the thick veil of my shock and fear, I noticed he was still panting. His eyes were wet and red. His mouth was strained. He looked like he had run a marathon. I had an impulse to go to him—to, like before, ask if he was okay. Of course, it stalled. It crashed and burned.

Hysteria is different than crying. Different, even, than a sob. It's like emotion bursting out. Volcanic ash, lava. Sounds poured from my chest, erupted out my throat, sobs and gasps and the pained sounds that dogs make when they're left alone. This was not from sadness, or even necessarily from fear. I just couldn't comprehend.

Nick started talking, quick and soft. "Please don't be scared. I'm not here to hurt you, Milo."

I sobbed louder, and as I watched, Nick sank to his knees—out of steam. I stayed standing, stayed crying until I couldn't cry anymore. Then I thought about the words he used. The emphasis. *I'm not here to hurt* you, *Milo.*

"Why are you here?"

Nick's body still shook, but his voice was steady, strong. "Survival."

I wanted to scream at him to stop talking in riddles! "What does that mean?" I asked desperately.

"Where I'm from—We share a consciousness," he told me, voice normal, like we were talking about anything. "Everyone in my…race—it's not even right to say 'everyone.' It's more like we're all different parts of the same brain."

I made a frantic, shuddering sound, and Nick rose strode toward me. I tried to run, this time, but my knees gave out; I fell back in the grass, and Nick stood over me.

"Milo, please. Don't be afraid of me—*please*." Every word he spoke was frightening. Looking at him scared me. "Please," he whispered, crouching down. Above his head, I saw the stars; they sparkled and flared as my tears rolled. "Don't be scared." He touched my knee, and I stared at that hand. An alien hand. An alien.

I had a sudden image of us in the party store, eating ice cream. I remembered hugging him and felt betrayed. I studied his face, looking for some physical sign that he was what he said he was. But all I could see were his eyes, deep brown eyes that made me feel even more off-balance.

"We need gold. My kind, we're like your Internet—in maybe 500,000 years. We're all connected. You may have heard of it described as 'hive mind.' We're not corporeal anymore, not really. It's—" he frowned, clenching his fist. "It's hard to explain. There are language limitations. But the core of us—our heart, you might say—We still need metal, a conductor. To conduct that much energy, we need gold.

"We've figured out how to make it last," he said. "We only need a small amount—a relatively small amount—and we have bacteria that make it. But we're so large. There are so many of us." He did air quotes around 'many,' subtext of a concept I couldn't begin to comprehend. "And what we're doing—compared to other beings, anyway—What we're doing is complex. We've sucked our planet dry, and we've mined others, too."

I felt dread creeping up my throat. They've mined other planets? Suddenly I realized that I might have been on the wrong side.

"Are you going to do that to Earth?"

He shook his head. "There's a system. We observe the planet, its inhabitants. If the life is intelligent, we leave it alone."

He had meant to soothe me, but all that I could think was: "If it isn't?"

Lips pressed tight. Eyes flitted down, into the grass. "If it isn't then…we come."

I stared at the warm hand on my knee. Somewhere in the distance, I could hear another helicopter. It seemed far away.

"What are you called?" I asked him hoarsely, and I could see his face relax, his eyes soften.

"We don't have a human name," he said softly. "We don't speak in language. Verbal language," he corrected. "But if you made it into a sound, it would sound like Russian."

I giggled a little wildly. Okay—a lot wildly. "You're lying. It's just so hard to believe!"

"I'm sure it is. But I'm not lying, Milo."

To me, he was. And as long as we were playing pretend, "I've got another question." Behind Nicks' head, the last wall trembled; I ignored it. "What… uh. What happens if the people—creatures. What happens if they aren't smart enough?"

He hesitated, which was all the answer I need. "Well how do you measure!"

"Several ways."

I sat up straighter, leaning on my arms; my palms pressed into the damp grass. "What about us? Humans? Are we okay? I mean, do we pass? We have to, right?"

He was silent for a long time, his face hollow and drawn, and I knew he had to be joking. "Nick, seriously! Obviously we're intelligent. I mean..." We had cars. Computers. The Internet.

"It depends," he said finally. "It just depends on how you calculate it. By traditional standards, maybe not."

My head buzzed. "So we're going to be exterminated?!"

"No. *No.* Well, it depends. It depends on a lot of different factors. Beings evolve so differently. The scale has to be re-imagined for all of them."

"Who re-imagines it?"

Nick looked down: heavy, shamed. "For this planet, me."

"You?" I felt relieved, then sick all over again.

"Me and... my partner."

"Where is he?"

Nick stared down at his tattered jeans, picking at a loose thread with the hand that wasn't swollen anymore.

"I was supposed to meet her," he said quietly.

Her. "So why didn't you?"

"Because," he said, and looked at me. "I wanted to see you."

CHAPTER TWENTY-NINE

I stared at Nick's face, re-playing his words, and I felt my pulse quicken.

"Me?"

His hair rustled in the breeze, coppery, beautiful, so human, like the oh-so-subtle tightening, then curving of his pretty lips. His gaze dropped to his leg; he was kneeling now, his arm propped on his knee. He fiddled with his shoe and glanced back up at me.

"I... care about you, Milo." I watched his face tighten, then relax, like a boat's sail flapping in an unknown breeze. His shoulders rose, then fell, and he finally brought his gaze back up to mine.

"I'm kind of your version of Christopher Columbus or... I don't know, Neil Armstrong. Except I don't go anywhere usually. I use our knowledge base to scan other planets. That's what I was doing when I saw you."

He stared at me, like he was trying to impart some great truth.

"It was approximately 66 days ago by how you measure time. You were at that big, flat rock. You were crying. I was over Golden, scanning and I... zoomed in, I guess you could say. I wanted to see things through human eyes, and I could simulate... a little bit. When I saw you..."

He shook his head. "I could see your sadness. Like a color. It was orange. Bright. Like... a candle in a dark room, but a hundred times as big. I was... intrigued."

"Intrigued..." I echoed.

He smiled softly. "We don't have feelings. Emotions. Not the way you do. Some of us are more susceptible than others. I... my function is to scout and assess. To do so I needed a certain separation from the rest. A certain... inquisitiveness?" He tried the word, then shook his head. "A certain interest, maybe."

His mouth tightened, and I could see his shoulders rise a little. "There's no easy way to explain it. And I'm not sure why you...had the effect on me that you did. I wasn't in a position to know the history of Us. I don't know if any part does. But it's possible that whatever we evolved from... might have related to existence in a way similar to humans." He shrugged. "I like to think something inside me, some residual... *humanity*, was drawn to you."

"And you just came?" I asked.

He nodded.

"And the others just let you?"

He blinked, those solemn brown eyes large—as he tried to explain. "I'm kind of... an important winkle on the brain," Nick went on. He smiled, totally humorless. "I'm kind of a big deal. There aren't many of us—the ones who seek resources. So I wasn't noticed...when I started watching you."

"I was supposed to go to New York. My partner was going—probably still is in Tokyo. But I changed course. I think I... Well, I kinda had you on my 'mind,' and right as I was coming in—coming into Earth, I mean—coming into consciousness, your human consciousness—I noticed a body being vacated. It was close to you, and just about the age I needed. Just about your age."

Against all reason, I felt a burst of warmth.

"I jumped in, without preparing. I was just going to see you. Just once, get a look at you," he said, smiling, almost silly. Then his torso tightened and he sped up. "I reworked the body, moved it to you, and I tried to jump inside. I brought all the data, all the knowledge that I needed with me. I'd programmed my mind in advance to know everything I'd need for Earth. Right down to the clothes. I'd created the suit for Wall Street. But using Gabe's body... Using a foreign vessel, one I hadn't studied..." He shook his head. "I messed up my consciousness, and I lost my memory completely."

He took a deep breath, then held out his hands to say, "All done."

I think other girls—more practical, maybe, or those who hadn't been spiraling downward for two straight years— would have been concerned about their friends, their families, and the billions of people they hadn't met yet, but who were living and innocent and...etc. All I could really think to ask, though, is: "Was I worth the trouble?"

My heart stopped until he smiled. "Yeah. Yeah, you were worth it. *Are*."

I stood up, feeling warm and fuzzy, feeling also the heat of the blaze a few hundred yards away from us. We needed to get away, but neither of us moved. We stood, staring at each other, both transfixed—and for such different reasons.

"So I guess we know why those people are after you."

"We do." His eyes bored into mine. "I need to get you

home."

"No! I can't let them take you."

He smiled sadly. "I don't think that will happen."

Well, duh. Of course not. Alien. The thought of it still sent a shock-wave through my paltry human brain.

"What are you going to *do*?" I asked. I couldn't imagine how anything worked now.

Nick shrugged. "Don't know."

"But you can do…like, anything, right?" There was another helicopter, its thrum-thurm-thurm getting louder, closer, but I couldn't get my feet to move. I felt rooted to the grass, rooted there with Nick.

"Not anything."

"But a lot."

Nick nodded.

"That's really weird. And cool."

"You aren't…angry?"

I shook my head. "Would it matter if I am? I mean, do emotions…" I didn't know what I meant.

Well, no, I did. I wondered if it was possible for him to like me. If when he said I was worth the trip, he meant as more than a specimen.

He stepped closer. "I feel things like a human when I'm in a human body; when my consciousness is human. The emotions are still…surprising, but they're potent."

He stepped even closer, put his hands on my waist, and gently turned me, pressing his chest into my back. I went limp and inhaled smoke and grass and him.

"There's something about you… Whichever form I'm in, I like you, Milo. I'm drawn to you."

I smiled, still feeling totally schizo. "I'm not too…

unevolved?"

"Not at all."

"None of this makes any sense."

And then it didn't matter. Nick jerked, and he dropped down over me, and I heard a bullhorn as I felt the grass and heard the guns and felt Nick moving off me, standing up and sweeping them away. I looked up and saw him struggling.

His eyes drooped shut as a handful of men and women landed several dozen feet away. He knelt down, arms spread over me, and darts flew at his back. One hit me, too. And I was heavy, so heavy.

Ella James

CHAPTER THIRTY

At first, when my eyes opened and I looked around the room, I thought I was on a band trip. I blinked up at the dappled hotel ceiling—just a little too low over my head. A quick sweep of the room revealed two double beds with paisley bedding; a cherry wood dresser, armoire, and entertainment system; and a royal blue armchair with a small, round footstool. Mirrors covered every wall. I found my reflection in the one across the room and, for an odd moment, wondered why no one was with me. Our school's head band director, Mr. Kline, usually stuffed us at least four to a room—five if there was space for a cot.

The table between the beds, bearing a small pull-chain lamp, a yellow pad, and a pen, should be littered with bags of gummy worms and empty soda cans. My heart-rate kicked up a notch as I realized something else was missing: curtains. The room didn't have windows. Weird.

I jumped out of bed in a panic, and before I could make it to the mirror, I saw the dirt smudge on my cheek, right by my lip. That brought the whole thing flooding back.

Nick. The people in the helicopters. The—*oh, boy*—Department of Defense. My rattled mind spun, remembering Nick when he'd been ill. I felt a burst of worry for him, followed by a rush of worry for myself.

I jogged to the door and tried the knob, knowing before I touched it that it wouldn't open for me. It didn't have a peek hole.

I peered into the long mirror beside the bed, trying to use my hands to block the light in the room and maybe see…I wasn't sure. Did I see shadows, moving around on the other side, observing? Maybe not.

The uncertainty was terrible. I knew there could be people behind one of the mirrors—that there was definitely a room behind one of them. But I didn't know where exactly it was, or if there was anyone in there now. Maybe they were out. Maybe there was just one grad student, and she'd fallen asleep at her desk.

Maybe there were half a dozen scientists.

I sank onto the vacant bed and looked down at my feet. I was missing my shoes, which meant someone had taken them off for me. I stood, again, in front of the mirror, searching my body for clues. I rubbed a sore spot on my neck, spotted a small, red ring there: where the dart had hit me.

I had to assume they had me in some kind of facility. Where?

"Nick," I called out. A few steps into some shadows along one of the walls revealed a small bathroom, utilitarian and empty except for two towels and three rolls of toilet paper. I saw a vent on the floor beside the toilet and noticed how tiny it was. The ones in the bedroom were the same: too small even for my hand.

I sucked a breath in, and my lungs burned—like the air was too thin.

Since Dad's death, I'd had a thing about confinement. I

thought it had something to do with picking out his casket. Mom had been so upset that day, I'd offered to go with her to the funeral home. Afterward I'd dreamed, for months, about the tiny cedar boxes, framed with impressionistic chrome. Wooden boxes, all dolled up—but boxes just the same. I remembered when Dad's casket had shut. Knowing it would never open again.

I turned toward the door, a buzzing bee in a bell jar.

I turned toward the door, and it swung open.

There was a glorious moment where I thought that I'd been saved. I thought Nick would stroll in, blow the house down, and whisk me away.

Then I recognized the woman: Ursula. I'd seen her only once, in the doorway of my house with the man named Sid, but I remembered her spiky, blonde pixie cut. She wore no makeup, but her hazel eyes were framed by long, long lashes—so long that I'd have thought they were fake, except that Halah had taught me to spot fakes.

As soon as her gaze hit mine, she smiled—a wide, lipstick'd smile that belonged on a commercial for all-day gloss.

"Ursula," she said, in an accent that sounded faintly Canadian. She stretched out her dainty hand, and I shook it, mostly because I didn't know what else to do.

I could tell right away that she wanted something from me. She treated me in a way that was reminiscent of an elementary school teacher on the first day of the year: with a slight firmness she tried to cover with a welcoming air.

"Why don't you sit?" She pointed toward the blue armchair.

I looked at it, then at the door, which had slammed shut

behind her. I looked down at my socked feet. "Um... where exactly am I?"

She glanced back at the door, and I could see her mouth twist slightly. "A hospital!" she said, a notch too loudly.

I frowned. I didn't see anything hospital-ish about my room. "Which one?" I asked.

"It's private."

I looked her over—thin black t-shirt, butt-hugging black slacks, lace-up boots straight out of *Deliah's* Magazine.

"And you're a nurse?" I asked.

"I'm Ursula—" she smiled again, thinly, "and I work for the FBI. We were called in when you were kidnapped by—"

"I was *kidnapped*?" I swallowed, realizing I had no idea what game to play with her. I screwed my face into confusion. "Who told you I was kidnapped?"

Her thin, dark eyebrows pinched. "Are you saying that you weren't?"

My stomach roiled. "I'm saying, who told you that?"

"Let's see..." She held out her left hand, ticking off points on her fingers. "Your mother has issued an Amber Alert. She claims that you were kidnapped. Your friends say you've been out of touch. And you were seen with Gabe DeWitt. We found you in your friend Sara Kate Mackris' cabin."

I nodded dumbly.

Ursula plopped down in the chair, sticking out her short, curvy legs and stretching her arms behind her neck. "We haven't found Mr. DeWitt yet, so I was hoping you could tell us what you know."

At that news, I felt a thick flip-flop in the back of my throat, like a frog rolling over, curling up. "You haven't seen

Gabe?"

Did that mean he'd gotten away, or had he—Oh, crap. Had he possibly…gone *home*?

I tried to think of a game-plan, but whatever they'd shot me with hadn't let up. I had no idea what would make the best story, so I folded my arms and looked down at my feet.

Ursula took it from there. She got up and grabbed the yellow notepad and started jotting notes in it, occasionally glancing up to ask me a question.

How did I know Gabe? (Band camp). Which year? (I didn't remember). What did he play? (Oboe). What did I play? (Piano).

"So you're good at piano?" she asked, chipper.

"I don't know," I said. "Not really."

"And Sara Kate Mackris? She's your best friend?"

"Sara Kate has nothing to do with this," I said. "She didn't even know we were going to her cabin. I didn't either, actually." I rubbed my head, deciding to pull a Nick. "I don't remember how we got there. Did you give me some kind of *drug*?" I held my hands out, widened my eyes like I was getting upset. "I don't remember anything!" I lied. My eyes teared, because I did remember, and I was beginning to feel the weight of terror. "I just want to see my mom."

Ursula got up, tucking the pad into the pocket of her pants like a waitress at Outback.

"I'll be back in just a little while, and we'll arrange for your release. Until then, if you need anything…" She handed me a small cell phone. "One will get you me."

I tried to dial out, but the phone wouldn't cooperate, so I spent the next half-hour trying not to hyperventilate. Once I got a handle on myself, I tried to assess the situation. It seemed pretty straight-cut, in a weird, fantastical sort of way. I understood now why they wanted Nick. Assuming this whole thing wasn't some bizarre reality TV show—which it couldn't be, I reasoned, because the story of Gabe DeWitt had been all over the real news—the government was after Nick because he was an—big gulp—an alien.

Extraterrestrial. That sounded a little nicer.

So Nick was an extraterrestrial, and I was guilty by association.

I thought about the Nick-related questions Ursula had asked me, about how I knew him. I decided the odds that Nick had gotten away from them were slim (I'd seen him crumple in the grass), so I figured they were questioning us both to see if our answers matched. That's what they usually did on TV.

I walked over to the door and tried the knob, and told myself I shouldn't be surprised when I couldn't get it open.

Just breathe, Milo.

Of course they wouldn't let me out—not yet. They weren't finished with me.

The challenge was making them think I knew absolutely nothing, and I was prepared to lie my pants off to accomplish that. I turned on the TV, settling on *Planet Earth: Seasonal Forests*, and thought some more.

They had Nick, and I felt sure that they would never let him go. They'd probably lock him up and study him forever, so it would be smart for Ursula to tell me that he'd disappeared. I had to pretend to believe them, and I had to feign ignorance, make them think that "Gabe" had wiped my memory with his superpowers. I had to get out, and I had to figure out how to help him.

How?

And if I was able to break him out, then what? A life of running from the cops? Not just cops. *Federal* cops. I realized I could even get killed. Of course I could.

I thought about Nick, I thought about aliens, and I felt a stab of panic. I'd always been scared of things like that, worried by the things I didn't know.

What I did know: Nick—Gabe, whoever—He liked me.

I stretched out on the bed, staring at the ceiling, and I tried to remember what he'd said.

There's something about you that's very appealing to me… Whichever form I'm in, I like you, Milo.

CHAPTER THIRTY-ONE

If Sid was a TV character, I would have said he was terribly cliché. With his charcoal t-shirt and cargo-style black pants, topped with black boots, and the whole outfit covering a *way* worked-out body, he was sort of a Power Ranger type. It didn't help that he had a crisp, accentless voice and a celebrity-style smile. Not that he smiled at me.

He strode into my room maybe four or five hours after Ursula left and told me I'd need to give a formal statement before they let me go, and to come with him. I didn't want to go, but I didn't really have a choice. Besides, anything was better than being locked in the "hospital" room.

The hallway Sid led me into looked like a hospital corridor—wide cement bricks under a coat of off-white paint, a low grayish ceiling and shiny tile floor—but that was only if you'd never been inside a government building. I had. Four years ago, when I was in seventh grade, I'd gone with Dad to the Department of Energy headquarters, in Washington D.C., for a meeting about a new part he'd invented for the turbines. That place had looked a lot like this one, right down to the crescent-shaped marks in the ceiling tiles.

I followed Sid as the hallway turned a few times, leading us past a bunch of big steel doors. Like in my room, the ceiling in the hall was low, and the air felt thin and cold and humid. I kept looking for windows, and after five minutes without seeing one, I got the creepy-crawly sensation that maybe we were underground.

I was still feeling a little sick at this thought when Sid pressed his palm into a glowing red pad by one of the doors. The lock clicked open, and I followed him into a tiny room, where I found a metal table and five chairs.

"Sit," Sid ordered. I complied.

He pulled out a chair across from mine and laid his arms out on the table. He glanced into a corner over my head, and I noticed a tiny wall-mounted camera in the corner behind him.

"Let me get right to the point, Miss Mitchell." His dark brown eyes bore down on mine, and he pressed his palms into the table as he spoke. "We've checked out your story, and we know that Gabe DeWitt never went to band camp. In fact, he doesn't play an instrument at all, according to his grandmother."

"His grandmother?" I echoed. Crap! Why had I ever told that lie? I straightened in my chair and tried to wear my best innocent look. "How well does his grandmother know him?"

Sid's stare was like a laser. "Gabe has a number of friends, and we've spoken with his schoolteachers." Sid's mouth pinched, and he inclined his head slightly more toward me, like we were co-conspirators or confidants. "Why did Gabe DeWitt visit you at your home, Miss Mitchell?"

Which time? I inhaled, trying to remember what Sid knew. Oh, right. I had *absolutely no idea.*

I shrugged. "He came by yesterday because we're friends. And," I added, on a whim, hoping to make myself seem more forthcoming: "he was scared."

"Afraid?" Sid said, one eyebrow arched. "Of what?"

I shrugged again, trying for the casual teenager vibe. "He said some weird stuff had been happening, and he was scared. That was all he said."

And *that* was the only card I was showing.

"Why did you leave with him?" Sid asked.

I stared down at my lap, then looked him in the eye and shrugged. "I really don't remember. I don't remember much except for waking up here."

"You're lying." Sid pushed himself up and stood over me, frowning. "You didn't know Gabe DeWitt until a week ago, when the two of you made contact after an astronomical anomaly crippled the Denver metro power grid. I think there's a reason that you're lying for him."

I blinked, stunned to silence.

Sid stuck his hand into his pocket. He held out Nick's whistle.

"What is this?"

I could feel the blood draining from my face. If Sid had the whistle, that meant Nick was definitely somewhere here. I tried my best to rebound. Shifted position, folded my hands in my lap. Rolled my eyes. "It's a whistle," I said. "Obviously."

Sid closed the whistle in his fist and crossed his arms. "You need to re-think your story, Miss Mitchell. When you decide to be honest with us, you'll be free to go."

I couldn't be honest with them. This left me stranded in my "hospital" room, which was at times called a hotel room, and one other time referred to as a holding cell.

I probably would have freaked, would have felt like a prisoner with no hope of escape, but Sid had left me in the care of the world's most ridiculous guards. Privately, I thought of them as the Reject Squad.

There was Ursula, whose shirts were indeed from the GAP, and who apparently owned stock in the company. When she sat in my room with me, she wore a hot pink MP3 player and sometimes hummed along with The Ramones. Then there was Diego, the blond-haired guy who'd originally shown up at my house with Sid, poking around in search of Nick—though at the time they'd claimed to be investigating the power outage.

Diego was, I quickly learned, popular with the ladies here at casa de gobierno. He had a shiny black new iPhone, and when he sat in the blue chair, he kicked his feet up and spent his babysitting time texting—usually Ariel, I thought.

Ariel had to be about my age. No more than a few years older—I was certain. Like Ursula, she was short and curvy; she had tiny, rubber-band-bound dreadlocks that stuck up from her scalp like broccoli florets. She, too, wore all black, but her shirts were slightly spandex, and her pants were entirely pocketless, so the outline of her booty was flawless. And all the better for wiggling in Diego's face.

On my second day there (I think it was the second day), Ariel took the early morning shift, and it was she who revealed to me the origin of everybody's names. She didn't have to do any explaining. She just commandeered the remote and settled on *Ice Age: The Meltdown*, and when we reached a scene that featured both the goofy-looking sloth (Sid) and the saber-toothed tiger (Diego), she giggled and muttered, "They should've been switched."

Sid and Diego. Ariel and Ursula: *The Little Mermaid.*
Doyyyy.

So this was the Department of Defense? A bunch of attractive new college grads with cheesy cartoon aliases?

Sometime in the afternoon, that first full day in prison, Diego arrived to switch shifts with Ariel. After the two of them made goo-goo eyes at each other, and I was pretty sure Diego made a swipe at Ariel's butt, Diego cocked his head back toward the door and said, "We're going on a field trip."

Great.

The field trip turned out to be an elevator journey to— *get this*—somewhere *eight* floors down, to a hallway that was thinner than the one I was living off of, in a wing where every area was partitioned off with walls that popped up out of the cement floors like spikes. Diego had to press his palm to touch-screens sometimes, and he had to swipe a barcode ID tag at others.

"Snazzy," I said drolly, and he winked. "I know. I'm a rock star."

He gave me his goofy grin, and I knew he was making fun of himself. I liked him a little more for it.

We passed through three of the big steel doors and one of the creepy, pop-out-of-the-floor partitions, and Diego led me into what actually did look like a hospital room. He gave a little wave, and dipped out as a long-haired nurse in light blue scrubs walked in. She looked about 30, but it was hard to say.

"Mary," she said, her elbow-length black pony tail bouncing as she nodded my way. She blew a bubble—I smelled Bubble Yum—and, in the thickest Boston accent I'd ever heard, she said, "Why don't you sit down on the table and I'll get your stats."

My stats?

I frowned, and she said, "Really. Hop up there, kid. I don't got all day."

I did as she asked and wiggled onto the table. My heart hammered as she took my blood pressure—"Heart rate's high. You scared a somethin'?"—and took my temp and got my weight and height.

"Why do you need all this?" I asked her, as she scribbled on her clipboard.

She shrugged. "I don't ask the questions around here. I'm just a tech."

"What kind of tech?"

Her brow scrunched. "What kind do ya think?" She gestured to her scrubs and waved me toward another metal door. I stopped.

"Where are we going? Where did Diego go?"

"I don't know about Diego. Back there's the MRI machine."

I was feeling a little shaky now, a little shaky and a whole lot trapped. I looked up at the ceiling and wondered how far down I was. How far under the earth. And where? I had no idea where I was.

"Listen," Mary said, pointing up. "It's better not to think of that. You do your MRI without a fuss, you'll be back in your kiddie cabana in an hour."

I took a deep breath and followed Mary through the next door.

In case you've never had an MRI: It's scary. The machine looks like a thick white tube with a plastic cot jutting out in front of it. Mary told me that the cot—or table, rather—would slide inside once I got on. I knew as soon as I saw it that I didn't want to. My legs shook as I ducked behind a curtain and peeled off my clothes, then donned a green and white striped gown. When I emerged, feeling weird and violated, Mary held out her palm, and I found a small white pill inside.

"Chew this, hop on the table, we'll get going."

I blanched. "I'm not taking that thing."

Mary sighed and plopped down in a plastic rolling chair. "That's fine by me." She folded her arms and gave me the evil eye.

I thought about my mother, about Dad. I thought about Sara Kate and Halah and Bree, and I longed to be back home. I thought about how impossible it would be to escape here. No, I corrected myself. It wasn't impossible.

I inhaled deeply and thought of Nick. I had to be strong. For Nick. Freaking out would get me nowhere. I needed to act compliant. Make my captors lower their guard. When they did, I would... what exactly?

I exhaled, inhaled again. "What kind of medicine?" I asked.

"It's cyanide." She blinked, deadpan. "Xanax, honey. You ever had a Xanax?"

In fact, I had. I'd been given one the morning of Dad's funeral. I knew about them anyway, because I'd seen them sold at school.

I looked around the room, at the wall-mounted rubber cabinets and the tiny counter crammed with cotton balls, swabs, needles and vials. I looked at Mary in her rolling chair. I couldn't sit in this room forever. I needed to get out, back to my room. I took the Xanax.

I stuck it in my mouth, and Mary handed me some headphones. She helped me get situated on the table—I squeezed my legs together, praying that she couldn't see my rainbow underwear—and after that, I could hear her voice over the headphones, over the low lull of classical music. Handel, I thought.

She explained that I'd have to stay perfectly still while she took pictures of my insides, and if I did, she'd try not to take more than an hour. An hour! Already, the machine's smooth walls felt like they were closing in on me. I nibbled on the pill, using my left incisor to break off a small piece, and spit the rest out, onto the table; the tiny piece rolled toward my left forearm.

"I'm getting started now. Don't move, hun. Just relax."

I shut my eyes, and behind the music, I could hear a mechanical hum—or maybe more a roar. I heard some clicking sounds and sensed the machine moving around me. It reminded me of a robot, and from there it was all too easy to think about an alien.

The miniscule amount of Xanax I'd ingested must have worked like a charm, because I was able to drift off into a kind of daydream land. I thought about Nick's arms around me at the decimated cabin, about the way he'd looked when he was sprawled out on my bed. I remembered how he'd been hurt—and how he'd healed himself. If they hurt him here, could he heal himself again? Was he even here? Would I find him if I tried? If I tried, would I get caught?

My reeling thoughts were interrupted by a sharp, familiar voice: Sid! He must've come into my room, because I could hear him through Mary's microphone. He said something in a low, hushed voice, and Mary murmured something in return. I opened one eye, trying to see them, but I couldn't see anything but the machine around me.

"Milo?" That was Mary. "You're doing good."

I didn't answer, and she said, "You sleeping?"

"Mmm."

I was starting to feel heavy and tired, but mostly I just didn't want to talk to her. Especially not if Sid was around. A few minutes later, Sid said something that made my drifting mind think that he was leaving. I fought to stay aware, but I was so sleepy. I dreamed about Diego coming in. He teased Mary, then told her something; I wasn't quite sure what. I heard her laugh, and he said, "Yeah, it's wild."

Wild? I had the hazy fear that they were going to get busy right there in the room with me. People around here seemed inappropriate like that.

Then Mary said: "Is he conscious?"

My heart tumbled.

I heard a rustling sound, like someone's hand over Mary's microphone. Then a cacophony of voices. My mind processed them a bit too slowly, so the sounds had the feeling of cars crashing in slow motion.

"...sounds rough..."

"...don't kill him..."

"...Never seen one of these guys before."

Then the bit I later prayed I'd dreamed: "...slice and dice..."

CHAPTER THIRTY-TWO

It wasn't Xanax. I was out of it, but that part of my mind that checked out all the other parts was aware that they hadn't given me a Xanax. I felt dizzy and weird, restless but too heavy to move, and when the MRI was over, some people got me out and put me on a stretcher. My lids were heavy—too heavy to lift—but I wasn't totally unconscious. I could feel my arms strapped down.

Everyone around me was talking, and the only thing I understood was "twilight anesthesia." I heard Ariel say something about "such tiny veins!" just before I felt a prick in my hand.

My head felt buzzy, like it was filled with singing crickets, and I couldn't figure out how to talk, but I could hear them, as the metal doors slid by—so slow—and, at the very same time, the rectangular fluorescent lights darted by, dizzyingly quick, over my head.

As my other senses dimmed, my hearing seemed more acute.

"So you think he's her boyfriend?" That was Ariel.

"Dunno," Diego said. "Could be."

Suddenly Ursula was there. My eyes were open, and I could see her bobbing up and down, saying something about,

"MRI was crazy!"

Whatever she was saying interested all of them. The gurney slowed, and they all looked at each other.

"I need to see," I heard Diego say, and seconds later it was just me and Ariel. She glanced at me—I could hardly see her through the shadow of my eyelashes—and, when she was confident I wasn't with it, she put her phone up to her ear. "Downstairs. Diego, you guys wait for me. I'm coming down. I know I'm not; I'm an *observer*. Oh," she said. "You mean *dooownstairs*?"

It sounded like she was talking in a code. I strained to understand, but fog was creeping over me again.

She laughed. "Like, forever, baby. He'll be down there forever. Unless E.T. phones home."

After that, I was somewhere else, and Sid was there. He kept asking me how I knew Nick, and I kept saying, "band camp." At one point, I saw Ariel's face—frustrated—and I felt another pin-prick in my hand. And I think Sid asked me if Nick was an alien.

I laughed. "That's insane."

And I'm pretty sure he asked me: "Are you human?"

No, dipshit. I'm a vampire, I thought. *I'm a vampire with bloody fangs.*

I giggled, "You suck at this."

Mary was there, hanging in the doorway, saying something about "…normal. Not like him."

I woke up mad.

Ursula was there, in the blue chair at the foot of my bed, and she was watching *Wheel of Fortune*. I squinted at the screen, and she shouted, "FAIRY TALE PRINCESS

PRIDE!'"

Princess Bride, I thought disdainfully.

I stared at her short, spiky hair, thinking what a moron she was. How was it possible that people like her were successfully keeping me in hotel prison? But they were—and re-realizing it brought on a fresh crest of panic. Which brought on a larger wave of panic as it dawned on me (for the dozenth time) that Nick was really an extraterrestrial (I'd started calling it 'ET'), and that there were ETs at all and I freakin' knew one, and that instead of peaceful discourse, the government had chosen capture and imprisonment. And they'd kept me around, too.

Suddenly it didn't seem real—that he was actually an alien. Not an ET—an *alien*. I looked out at Diego and Ursula and the flatscreen TV and none of it seemed real. But my hand was sore from the IV line in it, and my head throbbed, and I was finally feeling hungry…

My eyes watered. This was real. All of it was real. I didn't know how to swallow it.

Nick, an alien…

If he was an alien, why couldn't he talk to me inside my head? If he was an ET, why hadn't he broken out and saved me? What if he'd gone…home? What if I never got out? I felt momentarily betrayed; I had taken care of him, and I'd never known…anything. I hadn't known what—who I was dealing with.

But then I felt guilty. He was just Nick, and I cared about him.

From somewhere in the back halls of my mind, I remembered hearing something about Nick. Something…bad. Something that made me feel certain he had not escaped, made me feel desperate to escape and free him. I tried to remember what it was, but my mind was filled with nightmare images—abstract and completely without context.

Palms sweating, heart hammering, I sat straight up and blurted, "I want to go home."

Ursula turned her head, looking like a slutty college girl in her snug black outfit. Her eyes widened—she wasn't even smooth enough to keep her face neutral!—and she turned the rest of the way around to face me.

"Well, good morning, sunshine."

"Is it daytime?" I demanded.

"No."

"I want to go home," I said again, noticing, as I did, that I had plastic oxygen tubing in my nose and I was wearing a gown.

Ursula nodded, completely disingenuous. "You will—at some point."

"When?" I sounded bitchy.

She shrugged, looking slightly annoyed, and ran her palm over the tips of her hair. "It's not up to me."

I peeled the tape off my IV line and pulled it out, and did the same to the oxygen line, then hopped off the side of the metal bed and stepped toward the door. I don't know what I was doing; I guess I was freaking out.

"Milo, don't—"

At that exact second, Diego emerged from the bathroom, zipping up his fly, and I became aware that my butt was bare.

I jumped back into bed, dizzy as I jerked the sheet up to my chest.

"Whoa!" Diego held up his hands, but he didn't step

back into the bathroom.

"Milo! I told you—" Ursula started.

"No you didn't. You haven't told me shit!"

I was shaking—from fear and embarrassment and God only knew what else. As Diego and Ursula exchanged a faux worried expression and settled in front of the TV, I struggled not to cry. I thought Dad's death had been the hardest thing that would ever happen to me. I felt ten times more lonely and scared now.

On that note, I burrowed under my covers and curled into a ball, feeling self-conscious that my butt was facing out but needing to hunker down more than I needed my already ruined modesty.

I told myself to *think*, and when I couldn't come up with any plan I thought would work, I shed another tear or two and fell asleep out of sheer exhaustion.

I awoke after what must have been a shift change to the sound of Diego and Ariel arguing the merits of printed books. It sounded like Ariel had a Kindle—possibly it was even in her hands that second—and Diego thought "books should just be books."

Ariel was trying to tell him he could buy a book anywhere—"even right here, in the middle of a mountain, there is a bookstore."

Suspicions confirmed. And yikes: a mountain. I had a second to hope she was exaggerating, and then I remembered what I'd heard while I was out of it: how everyone had rushed "downstairs" to gawk at something Nick-related. Maybe Nick himself. How someone had said something that had made me think they would keep messing with him until they found out everything they needed to know. Not just messing with him—treating him like one of those cats we'd dissected in sophomore biology.

The horror that I felt at that—that someone might hurt Nick—Nick who had humored my inebriated friends and taken care of Annabelle, Nick who had held me so gently at the party and kissed me so sweetly on the stage—was indescribable, and I guess it kicked my mind into overdrive, because immediately I had a plan.

It was actually embarrassingly simple. I would, to use one of Dad's old Southern phrases, "play possum" until one of them, preferably Diego, went to the bathroom. Then I'd burst out of bed and pounce on the other one, preferably Ariel, and steal whatever they carried for defense. I hoped it wasn't a gun; then I hoped it was. Anything to help me escape and find Nick. And I *would* find Nick.

Not fifteen minutes after I came up with my plan, Diego ceded the argument—which had morphed into a discussion about newspapers, which had morphed into something more along the lines of a political debate. I could hear a shuffling sound, and Ariel said, "See how superior it is?"

Diego said, "If you're like, a book *addict*. 'Gotta have my Nora,'" he said in a high-pitched voice.

"Nora?"

"Nora Roberts? Isn't that what you gals like?"

"I don't know, Mr. Boss Man," she said, sarcastic. I was holding my breath now. "Do you like big trucks, big boobs, and beer?"

Diego laughed. "As long as the beer's big."

I wanted to scream, but I managed to lie still until I heard Diego walking toward the bathroom. I inhaled, exhaled, cracked my eyelids open. And saw Ariel leaning over a swanky new Kindle Fire with a little smile on her face.

I was quiet when I wanted to be. Had learned to sneak over S.K., who woke up when the central heat in Bree's house turned on, to get off the bed. So I was able to get up, and quickly, without Ariel noticing a thing.

I figured the fastest Diego would be back was thirty seconds, so I counted down in my head while I looked for something to hit Ariel with. I didn't see anything that was both blunt and light enough for me to lift. But I did see a syringe, and a vial that looked the same as the knock-me-out drug.

I tiptoed over, terrified that at any moment she'd turn around and spot me. I had just finished filling the syringe when something buzzed. I jumped, heart pounding, and she reached into her pocket. Cell phone.

She sat the Kindle on her lap and said, "Ariel," in a crisp tone that made her sound like a model worker.

I was shaky all over, but I didn't have time to waste. I walked as softly as I could, closing the distance between us while Ariel talked on her phone.

"Oh nooo. Yes, I've assisted with that before." There was a little pause, during which I thought my head might explode. Then she said, "Is it bad? Well, you know Ursula; she's squeamish. I have a stomach of steel." Another pause. My stomach roiled. "Same place? You *do*? Well, okay... She's sleeping, though. It's really not necessary..."

"Fine."

She snapped her phone shut just as reached the couch. She stood, turned, and her mouth dropped when she saw me.

I shrieked and jumped at her. I tried to jump over the

couch—I was aiming for her neck—but I didn't quite make it. I fell forward, and instead stabbed her in the leg.

She shrieked and kicked me, and I tumbled onto the floor. I jumped up as quickly as I could and charged. In retrospect, I'm pretty sure I was none too smooth, but I made up for it with cat-like fighting skills. I clawed her face and when she reached for a weapon in her belt, I kicked her in the shin and slapped the Taser out of her hand.

At that point I didn't have to do much else. The shot finally did its job, and she fell like a tall tree. I heard Diego shuffling in the bathroom, then say, "Arie?"

Every muscle in my body trembled with adrenaline. Taking big, shaky strides, I glided to the door and had the Taser aimed at crotch level when he stepped out. He jumped back, but the current caught him anyway, somewhere near the upper thighs. Diego cursed, then dropped down to his knees.

I turned and shot toward the door, realizing a few feet away from it that I needed someone's tag. Ariel was sprawled out, so I searched for the square bulge in her tight pants and stole hers. I didn't even have to swipe it. As soon as I reached the door, I saw a green light beside it flash, and when I tried it, it opened.

CHAPTER THIRTY-THREE

I dashed into the hall, half expecting Sid to jump out at me. I looked left and right. Which way had he taken me? I had no time to think about it. I went with my gut: right. I must have been running fast, but it didn't feel that way. I felt like I was in a dream, and I couldn't move my arms and legs fast enough. My gaze hopped from door to door and I held the Taser out, ready to defend myself—but no one came. I didn't even hear an alarm, which in a way made me even more nervous. I took another left, and then a right, before I realized *Sid hadn't taken me to an elevator*.

Baktag!

I turned a circle, dizzied by the stark white walls and the long line of identical metal doors. My heart was beating so fast I worried I'd pass out. I'd never find Nick! I'd never get out of here! I was wearing a butt-less gown!

And then I saw it—a tiny sign on the white-washed brick in front of me: **FIRE EXIT**, and beside it, a symbol depicting stairs. Elevators were usually beside stairwells, right?! I made like Wiley E. Coyote, following the signs through two more turns, and when I saw the elevators, I wanted to cheer.

There was only one problem: When I pressed the silver

"open" button, it beeped discordantly and flashed—in the unmistakable shape of a fingerprint.

I tried mine anyway. Then I waved Ariel's badge in front of it, and when that didn't work, I lunged into the stairwell. I had a hazy memory of a disembodied voice saying something about "zero." It was a crap shoot, but heading down was the only thing I knew to do. I ran down so many stairs that I started falling down them. And then they ended.

I shoved through a door, expecting a hallway, but I found myself trapped in a boxy room the size of a bathroom stall. In front of me was an elevator. Behind me, a camera.

Double baktag!

But I did feel energized, because I knew I had gone the right way; the lower floors were just like in the movies: the big stuff happened there.

I flipped off the camera, then zapped it with my Taser and rammed into the big, cold elevator door. Naturally, it didn't budge. I kicked it with my bare foot, waved Ariel's badge over the fingerprint pad. I jabbed my finger at it, and it responded with a series of shrill beeps. I pulled my gown shut in the back and turned a circle, starting to panic.

The door opened so fast I didn't see it happen even though I was looking right at it. One second I was looking at my smeared reflection in the steel, the next I was staring down two women—a tall African-American with a sharp, straight nose, pretty eyes, and a dark green "guard" getup and...Ursula?

I opened my mouth, starting to say something; then I realized I should turn around and RUN. I got about half a step before the tall guard grabbed me. She was so adept she didn't even really hurt me, just captured my biceps and whirled me around, setting me down almost gently in the doorway of the elevator, where Ursula snatched the Taser from my hand and fired in my direction.

She must have been a lousy shot, because it didn't seem to work.

The guard tapped me on the back, but her tap was something special: it sent me flying into the back wall of the elevator. My forehead hit it, I fell down to my knees, and when I touched my head, my palm came away bloody.

Ursula delivered a shockingly vicious kick to my hip; it hurt so bad I doubled over, literally seeing stars. The next thing I knew, superwoman (that'd be the guard) had me on my feet, pinned in front of her. I could smell strawberry lip gloss, which made the whole thing doubly surreal.

"You're such a fucking moron," Ursula said, and all I could think was that she had read my mind; I'd called her a moron in my room. Then I went cold; what if she was an alien, too? What if she was Nick's partner?

I must have given her a look, because she laughed and said, "Jesus, I won't bite you."

"I may." That was super-stealth, who gave a little laugh.

"You can't keep me here! I didn't do anything," I shouted, and Ursula laughed. Then the door opened and they marched me out.

We were in another hall—and this one was *really* cold. I stumbled out, still in super-stealth's grasp, and surprised to find how little I cared about my bare butt. I turned to Ursula, desperately hoping to appeal to her human side—*if there was one*.

"Ursula, *please*! I just want to go home! I'm sorry! I panicked!"

We were moving now—super-stealth was pushing me along; Ursula strode in front of me, walking backward as she leered my way. "Why'd you go down instead of up?"

Super-stealth had been tightening her hold on me, and by now my wrists were aching. Blood from my forehead dripped into my eyes. I could feel my pulse drum in the wound. I jerked forward. "Let me go!"

"Okay."

She let me go, and I ran like a kid in a carnival funhouse; Ursula caught me easily, throwing me over her shoulder like I wasn't almost her size. I thought how weird it was, that Ursula actually had turned out to be a *badass*. I even felt a shot of embarrassment: my ego, rearing its head even over pain and terror.

I couldn't see much—my face was smashed against Ursula's mid-back—so when I heard Sid's voice, I thought I was hallucinating. Then Ursula stopped. She put me down, and I turned.

Sid was standing in the hallway, arms crossed, wearing a slick black suit and a purple tie.

"Thank you, officers," he said. "I'll take it from here."

Super-stealth made a little *awe* noise, like she was sad her fun was over, and Ursula gave me an exaggerated pageant princess wave. I looked up and down the hall, assessing my odds of escape. But I knew they were nil. I had screwed up—big time.

Sid didn't even bother to use force. He closed his hand around my forearm, passed me a neatly folded napkin—"Your head is bleeding, Miss Mitchell"—and led me into a little room with two chairs and a card table.

My stomach roiled. What a fool I'd been. To even think

I could do this. To jump into things without a better plan. Then I noticed the wall. The large window. I could see Nick on the other side.

Whatever Sid said first, I didn't hear it. My eyes were glued to the gurney, where Nick lay on his back. His body was wrapped in white sheets. Under them, his arms were crossed over his chest, like a mummy. Two thick leather restraining belts crossed his mid-section and ankles, strapped so tightly they made indentions in the sheets. A brown-haired, brown-eyed man in a long white coat stood to his left side, beside an IV pole, and as I watched he leaned over and started messing with an IV in Nick's neck. That was a central line, used for Serious Business; the interior end went all the way into Nick's heart.

I'd seen a central line before. I'd seen another person that I loved in this position, and seeing Nick like that...it made my legs feel weak.

My gaze canvassed his small, white room, looking for an out. But there wasn't one. We were stuck here, both of us—so I turned my eyes back to his face.

It looked so... different. For a stupid second I thought maybe he'd ditched Gabe's body and turned into "himself" but that was totally irrational, and anyway, if I squinted I could still see some resemblance.

So strange how when something awful hits you, your brain slows down like an overloaded computer. It took me a long time to figure out what was different: small things. His lips, always nice and smooth and often moving, smiling—they were badly cracked, with a blood smear in one corner. His jaw was bruised and swollen twice its normal size, which

225

gave him an uneven appearance. The rest of his face looked a little puffy, too, which made his nose look thinner. His closed eyes looked dark and sunken, in that way very sick people's eyes can look. And his forehead... I clenched my jaw. He had stitches across his forehead—a long train track of them that cut into his beautiful auburn hair. Of everything, it was his hair that made me cry. It looked so clean and perfect...so soft.

I remember the brown-haired man's hands—short and wide. How the rubber gloves were stretched as he depressed a syringe into the central line. How I wanted to kill him, because whatever he'd given to Nick *hurt*.

Through the darkened glass, I saw him moan. He tried to curl up; his shoulders pulled up, toward his ears, and his knees rose just slightly, though the strap held his legs down effectively. The brown-haired man knelt, doing something I couldn't see, and Nick arched back again, this time splitting open some of the stitches over his eye.

I remember my head got hot—the whole thing, very hot—and after that I was sitting in a chair, and Sid was leaning over me with his hands on the chair's armrests, and he was talking but I couldn't hear him. I looked past him, at the window—and that's how I saw the hand behind Sid's back. He was holding a Taser, and as he spoke, he brought it closer and closer...until finally it was in my sight and I brought my knee up hard under his crotch.

It connected with a satisfying crunch, and as he swore I rammed into him. It had been a while since I believed in God, but that day I knew that he was with me, because Sid's wrist bent in just such a way so that the Taser's fire went into him. He shot himself right in the pec, and then he fell back, much harder than you would expect from a typical Taser. Still, Sid was strong. He sat up, so I *kicked him in the face.*

Still riding my own wave, I grabbed a chair and knocked him in the head, then grabbed the Taser and ran out the door we'd come in and into the one I'd seen when I'd looked in on Nick. I shouldn't have been able to open the door to his room without someone else's fingerprint, but when I reached it, the pad lit up and I rushed in like an avenger, like someone in the movies, and that was good because another white-coat had come, and she was tightening Nick's binds. When I Tased her and she fell back, she had big eyes and a shocked, wide-open mouth.

Maybe they had cameras—maybe reinforcements were coming at that very moment—but I took my chances. I grabbed the felled woman and dragged her into a corner, where I stripped her of her blue surgical hair net and spent what felt like an hour wiggling the lab coat off her. The whole time, I burned for Nick. I was frantic to touch him, desperate to hold him. But my panic kept me on point. I swept my hair into the hat, pulled on the coat, and buttoned it before running to Nick's bedside. His eyes had opened; they were tired, but fixed on me.

I reached for his hand and felt a burst of air. The door behind Nick's bed flung open, and the brown-haired man walked in with Ariel, who was dressed in a similar surgical cap and coat, and wheeling some kind of machine.

I flung my arms up, and in a high-pitched voice, said: "We've got to get him out now! Move him to quarantine!"

They looked confused, then angry. The man said, "Who the hell are you?" and I could see it dawn on Ariel.

She rushed forward, and I was ready with my Taser. I

got her in the ear, and she staggered forward, then face-planted on the floor. The man was on me, wielding his own Taser, but when he jabbed it at me, nothing came out. I got him right between the legs. He howled, and I felt vindicated on Nick's behalf.

If it had only been the two of them, I could have handled it. But just that second, two others barreled in. I caught a brief glimpse of a man with grey hair and a woman in a white coat, and then something small and fast whizzed past my jaw and I screamed. I lunged for the bed, determined to free Nick, and the man grabbed my hair. I don't do anything to him, but as I wheeled around, I think my elbow might have hit him in the eye. He cursed, and loosened his grip on my hair, and the woman tackled me at the knees. I hit the floor hard. Pain sang through my back, and then she was being lifted off me.

I saw the man's face—wild eyes, twisted lips—and then it disappeared. The ceiling wobbled, I blinked, and I found myself looking up at Nick.

Chapter Thirty-Four

"Milo." The word was such a sweet caress, but we didn't have time for indulgences. Nick grabbed my hands and pulled me up. He pressed his mouth into my hair, and I could feel the warmth of his breath, and then we were running. I noticed the older man's leg twitch as Nick pulled me through the doorway, but I wasn't worried. Nick was up!

We dashed down the hall, toward the elevator, and alarms started shrieking. It sounded like more than one, and I wondered if one of them was aimed at Nick, because he flinched and pressed on his ear.

"What's—"

Suddenly the lights went out and the ceiling began to flash red; there were little red lights embedded at the top of each wall, the rows of them like lights on movie theater aisles.

Behind us, I could hear pounding footsteps, but Nick was moving fast, pulling me with him. I saw a blur of figures up ahead; I saw a red light, like a laser, and then I felt a burst of force and the path in front of us cleared. I smelled something sulfuric, I stepped on an arm; my legs felt weak and stiff, but Nick grabbed my hand, "C'mon! It's okay!"

A shadowed form swung out the door of one of the little

rooms, and Nick bounced back, into me. Then he dropped my hand. I heard a puff of air and heard a groan, and someone fell and it wasn't Nick because he had my hand again.

We ran.

Near the elevator—I thought we were near the elevator—we ran into a wall, a steel wall I didn't remember seeing before, the government equivalent of spikes in a road-block. Nick reached out and it crumpled, tinkling as it scattered on the floor like a broken mirror. As we started moving again, I noticed Nick was panting.

"Are you okay?" I cried over the sirens.

I could feel him nod.

He was guiding us to the elevator, but when we got to the area where it was, Nick grabbed my arm and stumbled back, then slapped the wall beside a fingerprint reader; it flashed and the door clicked open. He pulled me inside, and the door closed right before three or four sets of feet dashed by.

"Are you alright?" I hissed.

"Just... need to... rest." He was on one knee, rubbing his temple with his hand.

"What did they do to you?" I asked.

"Just... tests and stuff." He forced a small smile, then stood and pulled me out into the hall. This time, we went the opposite way; in the flickering red light, Nick nodded at a stairwell. We ran into it, and we climbed a few flights hand in hand. Tired as he was, Nick was still pulling me. I was feeling almost relaxed, glad we were covering ground, lulled by the pounding of our footfalls, when a door opened off one of the floors and Sid stepped out.

He had two long, cattle-prod like sticks in his hand, each crackling with current. I felt ill, but Nick just flicked his fingers, and Sid slammed against the wall, falling to the floor in a heap.

We ran past, but I remembered Nick's whistle.

"Crap!" I turned and dashed back to Sid. I found it in the first pocket I checked, and when I ran back to Nick, he was crouching. He stood quickly, giving me another tight smile, and we were gone.

We climbed and climbed. My legs shook terribly. My muscles tingled and my lungs burned. I didn't think we'd ever make it to...where? How far was high enough? I didn't even know.

The flashing lights and shrill buzzing were making me feel dizzy. Nick didn't seem too steady, either. I was starting to feel faint when he pulled me through a door and we were in a long, white hall—completely silent, with gray carpet and round wall globes and neat little clusters of leather chairs; peaceful and ordinary, like any corporate office in America.

Ella James

Chapter Thirty-Five

Nick must have had a sense of where our captors were, because he led me to a trio of chairs around a table with a potted plant, and we sat down. He leaned over, grabbed my hand; his wide eyes searched mine. "Milo...did anyone hurt you?"

Tears welled in my eyes, and I felt silly, glancing down at my stolen lab coat and raw, bare feet.

"I'm okay." I met his eyes. "Are you?"

He nodded, then looked over at the plant and rubbed his hair—where, I noticed, there were no stitches. In fact, his whole body was completely flawless and he was wearing a fresh pair of scrubs. "They...uh, they had some stuff rigged up to throw a wrench in some of my...um, plans."

"Like...?"

"I couldn't feel you." I arched my brows, and he took his hand from mine; he wiped his palms on his knees, looking almost nervous. "Usually I can...kind of sense you. I mean, since I saw you again down there... And before then, at the cabin... I knew I could do it. But they did a couple of different things, to be sure I couldn't get to you that way. So I didn't know...how you were."

His little speech was wrought with awkwardness, and

finally I realized why.

"So you can get away from them. Clearly. But... Are you saying you were worried about me... so that's why you didn't break out?"

He nodded, suddenly reaching for my hand. He traced it with his fingers. "They told me a lot of things about...your condition. I didn't really believe them, but..." He shrugged.

"So you just let them..." I trailed off, now feeling my own awkwardness. In fact, the awkwardness around our little table had pretty much quadrupled.

I looked at Nick. The alien. Who liked me. The alien who'd played lab rat for me, because apparently they'd used me as a threat. Which meant....the people here knew he cared about me.

"How'd they know to mention me?"

He was looking at the floor, his fingers still tracing circles on my palm. His eyes flicked up. "In the beginning... When that stuff they shot me with wore off. It was a big dose... really big, but I wasn't asleep for very long. But it was long enough... They said they'd—" his throat worked— "that they killed you. And they had some stuff hooked up so they could tell...it bothered me."

"Wow." My cheeks burned, and I almost pulled my hand away, but Nick's fingers captured mine.

"I freaked you out." His gaze implored, those brown eyes oh so serious. "It was worth the risk. On the off-chance that they meant what they said. I just wanted you to be safe, that's all."

I nodded. There was a big knot in my throat, one that was made up of shock and fear and gladness. I didn't know how to do this with Nick, but then again, I didn't think I would with anyone.

He was reaching for my hair, and my mind was spinning fast with thoughts of him and where we were, and as his warm palm touched my cheek I wanted to kiss him, and I wondered how he knew no one would find us here.

It must have been my seventh sense again, because as soon as I thought it, Nick jerked back. He snatched me up and pulled me over to the wall, and the stairwell door flew open. A swarm of people in black jumpsuits poured into the hall.

Nick shut his eyes, and I could have sworn I saw him flicker... à la hologram. I felt light and...fizzy, like a soda. And then I heard one of them say my name, and the fizzy feeling left. Someone gave a war-like shout, and they were on us, guns raised, crosshairs beaming.

"If I were you, I wouldn't move."

A few people parted, and Diego grinned at me.

I could tell by the way the people around him moved that Diego was in charge, and I realized with a shock that maybe I'd been wrong about the pecking order here. Sid had seemed more...forceful, and he'd questioned me and peeped in on my MRI, and he'd appeared to be in charge of Diego when I'd seen them at my house. But Diego was the one who'd moved in and out of my room with seemingly no schedule; he'd acted confident and cocky the whole time, flirting shamelessly with Ariel and Ursula, always giving me the feeling that he knew something I didn't. And while I'd taken Sid out without much fuss in that room beside Nick's, I'd only managed to get Diego because he'd been zipping up his pants...

His smile widened, like he was having the time of his life, a cowboy in a real Western. In one hand, he held something that looked like a cross between a sawed-off shotgun and a futuristic stun-gun; I followed its green sight to Nick's heart.

He winked at me, nodded at Nick. "Well hello again, Gabriel. I heard you took out a couple of my agents."

Took out…? Did that mean…

Diego took a step toward us, waving the gun, his hazel eyes on Nick. "Why don't you two come in here with us." He nodded at a door several feet away; it was wider than the others, metal painted brown, and as he nodded at it, the people around him got all up on Nick and me, and they guided us—at gunpoint—into what appeared to be a gym.

Nick tried to keep himself in front of me. I noticed his left eyelid twitching and worried he was too tired to fight. What if he couldn't get us out of this? I could try, but I didn't even have a weapon.

I looked around the room—gym. It was filled with equipment that I'd seen before on the Golden Prep football practice field, plus some more stuff that looked like it came from a work-out center, and little stations that looked like mini obstacle courses.

Diego leaned against some kind of balance beam, his gun once again pointed toward Nick. This time, he looked at me. "What were you thinking, Milo?" I detected a trace of Southern accent, an odd reminder of my dad. "Did you think we'd just let you walk out of here with *that*?" The word was crisp and damning. His eyes on Nick were hot enough to scald.

"Your boyfriend's property of the US of A. We've got

exciting plans for him." He smiled, and, scanning the group, I spotted another smile I knew: Ursula. "Our plans for you were more…mild, but I'm not sure we can roll with them now. You're on the wrong team, you know that?"

I glanced at Nick; he glanced at me, his eyes on mine just a second too long—long enough for me to see how tired he really was. I reached into the coat's pockets. I wanted to disappear. I wanted both of us to disappear. I balled my hand into a fist, and something brushed my knuckle. Right away, Nick's head whipped around, his gaze going to the pocket, like the whistle called to him. His eyes narrowed, only for an instant. Then he dipped his head toward me and mouthed, "Blow it."

Had someone else noticed his instructions? Had I been unsmooth pulling the thing out of my pocket? I would never know. A shot rang out, and I saw a burst of green over Nick's chest. His hand flew to his heart, and I blew the whistle.

Ella James

CHAPTER THIRTY-SIX

When I opened my eyes, I had the feeling some time had passed. I felt disoriented, wobbly. I blinked once, then twice, before I realized...everyone was frozen. Diego's lips were mashed together, his arm raised, his gun's nozzle pointed slightly up, as if a shot had just been fired. Everyone around him was halted in mid-motion. No, not halted... they were moving very, very slowly.

I whirled to Nick, feeling ill at what I thought I'd see, but he was reaching out for me. Behind him, I saw a dark, round shadow I soon realized was some kind of bubble.

He grinned. "Their time is suspended, but we're in another universe." He waved his hand up and over, and I followed it, shocked to see we really were inside a big, egg-shaped shadow thing. I followed the line of it, trying and failing to discern its texture. I followed it around and down, until my gaze bumped into someone new. She scowled and crossed her arms, and Nick said, "Milo, my partner... Vera?"

Nick squinted, and I followed his gaze back to "Vera," who I quickly noticed was wearing a bright red dress that touched the floor and hung behind her, rippling along the sides like teased ribbon. Vera Wang. The front cupped small boobs and led up to her milky throat, where a fluffy, toile strap wound around her neck.

I realized suddenly that she was Asian. Japanese, I thought. He'd said that. *My partner was going to Tokyo.*

I was still lost in thought when Vera opened her mouth and fast, soft Japanese bubbled out like water in a brook.

"… .. .. ….. .. ..! .. … ….. .. … .. . …!"

I had a slight idea of what she was saying. I knew it was Japanese because S.K. was learning Japanese, and I recognized maybe three of the words "Vera" said.

I watched Nick open his mouth and reply in Japanese so fluent he sounded like a native. He sounded angry. "….. .. ..! .. … .. … .. . …! .. ..!"

Vera scowled, her slender eyebrows drawing together under a line of stylish bangs. "… .. . …!"

I stomped. "In English!"

Vera turned to me, her eyes like daggers. "We have to go." The bubble stretched toward the door, and we set out into the hall.

Vera's look was not one I saw often, so she didn't fit my standard definition of beauty, but beautiful she definitely was. She had shoulder-length black hair that hung in layers around her heart-shaped face, and her soft bangs defied everything I'd ever thought about hairstyle coolness. She reminded me a little of Rinoa, one of the characters in *Final Fantasy* back in the day when S.K. and I had been obsessed with it.

She was dainty and very graceful, but she was also aggressive and impatient, stalking out in front of Nick and me the second we got into the bright hallway.

The hall was still buzzing with people: men and women

in dark-colored clothes, many clutching guns and speaking into ear-pieces. It was creepy watching their wide eyes move ghostly slow around the hall, knowing they were looking for us…and there we were, invisible right in front of them. Vera led the way to the nearest stairwell and started marching up. I wondered, as we walked, how she had made the bubble. Or had she done it? Maybe it was Nick and her being in the same place. I didn't think so, though.

Nick and Vera talked more as we moved; Nick's hand stayed hovering behind my back, and when I slowed, he slowed with me. Vera would protest, and Nick would say something else to her in Japanese. My head spun: slightly jealous of the beautiful Vera who understood everything about Nick, still terrified we wouldn't make it out, worried about what would happen if we did. I felt out of place as well, a fish out of water, the only Earthling…

Nick seemed to sense my unease. His fingers tickled my back, and at some point on the stairs he took my hand again, even though holding hands made it harder to keep up with Vera. The higher we got, the more people we started seeing in the stairwell. These were dressed in suits and clutching papers, briefcases, Blackberries. I wondered what time it was. I had lost all sense of…everything.

I started noticing that the people we passed were moving more quickly. Vera moved more quickly, too. Her dress flounced around her pale, toned legs. My legs started feeling like rubber.

"You all right?" Nick murmured.

I nodded, lying.

I felt completely overwhelmed. A man passed by close enough for me to touch; his arm swung beside him, almost at "real" speed. A woman, maybe in her mid-20s, scampered by; she didn't even seem slow.

Vera led us onto a floor, where people stood around dry erase boards, pointing and talking and dialing numbers into phones. Nick explained that we were going to the elevator.

"How do you know?" I asked.

He arched his brow and tapped his forehead, and my stomach clenched. We got into an elevator with a big-boned man who was looking at his watch. He scratched his face, picked at his ear, shuffled his feet.

The elevator opened into a room with windows. I saw cars and pavement, and then sound returned to the world. Suddenly dozens of eyes snapped to us, and Nick said, "Run!"

We didn't stop until we were standing in a cluster of firs on the side of a mountain. I couldn't tell what state we were in. Colorado? Wyoming?

Nicks' arm went around my back, holding me close. We were all breathing hard.

Vera looked at Nick. "Can we go?"

"What?" I said, shaken.

She didn't even look at me. "Clearly they have not passed." She rolled her eyes. "The planet is good for mining gold." I grabbed Nick's hand, suddenly shaking again.

Vera laughed. "Did you make friends with one?"

Nick glowered. "Vera, we need to talk about this."

She balked. "What?"

"I think you're wrong."

"I am never wrong."

"I disagree."

Her eyebrow lifted. "I'm not going to save this planet

just because you have some sick thing with a lower life form."

"I'm not a lower life form!"

"And she speaks. So *discordantly*." Vera reached into her dress pocket and pulled out a red whistle. My head felt hot. "It's time to blow these, *Nick*." She sneered his name.

Nick was holding his, cradling it in his palm like so much possibility. Vera brought hers to her mouth. Nick's fist closed, as if he wanted to crush his. When he couldn't, he gave Vera a meaningful look, dropped it on the ground, and stomped until it cracked. Vera crossed her arms and glared. Then she knelt to grab it, held it up, and blew across it. The whistle reassembled, and she brought it to her lips.

Ella James

Books by Ella James:

Stained (Stained Series Book 1)
Stolen (Stained Series Book 2)
Chosen (Stained Series Book 3)
Exalted (Stained Series Book 4) – Coming September 2012
Here (Here Trilogy Book 1)
Trapped (Here Trilogy Book 2) – Coming October 2012
Before You Go

Learn more about Ella and her books at
www.ellajamesbooks.blogspot.com and friend her on
Facebook at www.facebook.com/ellajamesbooks

Ella's eBooks are available at Amazon.com and BN.com.

Made in the USA
Lexington, KY
06 March 2013